HAMBURGER FOR ONE

HAMBURGER
FOR
ONE

RON UNDERWOOD

iUniverse, Inc.
Bloomington

Hamburger for One

iUniverse books may be ordered through booksellers or by contacting:

iUniverse
1663 Liberty Drive
Bloomington, IN 47403
www.iuniverse.com
1-800-Authors (1-800-288-4677)

ISBN: 978-1-4502-8142-3 (sc)
ISBN: 978-1-4502-8143-0 (ebk)

Printed in the United States of America

iUniverse rev. date: 12/28/2010

CHAPTER 1

The bright Florida sunshine soaked the beach as far as the eye could see, and each ray of sun seemed to bathe and gently caress the sand. Scores of carefree tourists jumped and played, relishing the fact that they were able to at least temporarily escape the cold, the snow, and their real lives. Millions of shells raced in and out with each wave as it arrived on the shore and then quickly retreated, making way for the next wave that would surely follow. Evan stretched his toe into the water and captured several small shells, not allowing them back into the Gulf. He realized how easily a life can be forever altered by outside forces; and despite the beautiful, relaxing setting, the emotions again overwhelmed him, and he remembered what had brought him here.

He stood ankle deep in the cool gulf water and then looked down the beach in both directions, realizing that one path was equally as good as the other, and he began to trudge along. He mused at the pelicans circling the water in their constant search for food, followed closely by ever-growing numbers of seagulls, apparently too lazy to search on their own and quite willing to let the pelicans do the hard work for them.

Another fifty yards down the beach, Evan was hit in the shin by a stray Frisbee. He could easily have seen it coming his way if he had been paying attention, but he was lost in his thoughts and was startled when it hit his leg. The child closest to him ran a couple steps in his direction and then stopped suddenly. "Sorry about that," he stated sheepishly.

Evan smiled and hurled their toy back to them. "No problem." He walked on, and he wished that controlling a harmless beach toy was all he had to think about. He veered onto a wooden pier and made his way to the farthest point, where he sat with his legs hanging over the edge. He could feel the sun on his shoulders, and he knew he would suffer the next day when the sunburn fully set in. For the moment, however, the heat felt very good, and Evan dipped his feet into the cool water beneath him. No answers were coming. He had tried, or at least he believed he had tried, but he had become far too familiar with the constant knot in his stomach. He knew that knot was the result of his dreams and plans being suddenly pulled out from under him without any real explanation.

Should he have been more prepared? Were there signs that he either missed or ignored? He kicked his legs harder in the water as if the churning and splashing would relieve some of his frustration. He wanted very much to scream as loudly as he could, but he knew he wouldn't do that. He was always too much in control of his emotions to ever just let go like that, especially in public, so he just sat staring blankly out at the endless water. His legs stopped kicking, and everything was again calm at the end of the pier, everything except the thousands of confusing thoughts that would not stop swirling around Evan's mind. He mumbled quietly to himself. "Isn't absence supposed to make the heart grow fonder, and aren't marriages supposed to last until death do you part?"

After a few more minutes, he made his way off the pier and back down the beach. The laughter of happy families drowned out the sounds of the jet flying overhead. He looked up, squinting from the bright sunshine, and as he stood and watched the plane vanish into the distant clouds, his cluttered mind wandered back three years to another plane he had longingly watched disappear into the sky.

The emotions of that earlier day were strong and long lasting for Evan. He had had no real way to prepare himself to deal with them; yet he knew the feelings, emotions, and memories of that day would never leave him. The awe-inspiring sight of nearly two hundred spouses, children, parents, and friends hugging, weeping, and cheering had overwhelmed Evan in ways he had never anticipated they would.

The uniforms and formations had been impressive, and those in uniform did their best to convey pride and enthusiasm in hopes of reassuring those family members staying behind. Most of the farewells had been taken care of before that day, so a lot of the visiting had been nervous small talk and light-hearted jokes about what to expect in the months ahead. The truth was that no one knew what lay ahead, either for those leaving or for those staying. Very few people there had ever before watched a spouse or a child go to war, and it was certainly not something Evan had ever imaged going through; but Rachel, his wife, was standing in the formation with the rest of her fellow soldiers, preparing to leave for a year of service in the Iraq war.

Evan reached the end of the beach, and the aromas from the sidewalk cafes began to get the best of him. It suddenly occurred to him that it was the middle of the afternoon, and he hadn't eaten anything all day except airline pretzels. The sun was still soaking the entire landscape, so Evan chose a table with an umbrella shading it. The temperature was still incredibly pleasing to him compared to the frigid air he had left at home, but his legs and shoulders enjoyed their break from the direct contact with the sun's rays. It was only when his body was away from the sunlight that he became fully aware of how sunburned he already was. He silently grinned to himself that winter sunburn was far better than the cold and ice he had left only hours earlier.

The food was delicious, and the atmosphere helped Evan break out into a momentary smile. Maybe this was why he had just packed a bag and gotten onto the plane. He looked around and wondered how anyone could feel bad in a place like this.

CHAPTER 2

F our years earlier, Evan and Rachel had shared their vows in front of their families and friends. Hope and optimism flowed everywhere with the belief that they had finally found the missing piece to each other's life puzzle. They had dated a couple years, relishing the company of the other, and for their inner circle it was always a matter of when, not *if* the two would get married.

The honeymoon had been incredible—a full week of sightseeing, golf, beaches, and romance. Intimate dinners had capped each day as the two quickly made the adjustment to fully sharing their lives as well as the same last name. It all seemed so promising then—a future together without any limits, a chance to joyfully grow old with that one other person destiny meant for each of us to find and share everything with. The first five months were a continuation of the honeymoon, and there were a thousand reasons for continued optimism regarding their marriage. The sixth month, however, began what turned out to be the first step in an irreversible journey in the wrong direction.

It was a warm, sunny Labor Day, and the weather was perfect. Summer was slowly walking itself to its exit, and the first signs of autumn were approaching the same door. Evan and Rachel spent a leisurely morning waiting for the afternoon to arrive so they could head to the cookout. A peaceful afternoon with family and friends seemed a great way to celebrate the end of an exceptional summer. Yard games and cheerful conversation filled the backyard, and the pile of empty beer cans grew larger by the hour. None of the dozen or so people there even spoke of work or problems, and the afternoon slowly wasted away to everyone's satisfaction amid laughter and smiles. Then Rachel's cell phone rang, and time stopped. Evan knew that something important and unusual was happening just by the expression Rachel suddenly wore on her face. He had never seen such a look of wide-eyed urgency before in his wife's expression, and he was instantly concerned and curious. By the time she put her phone down, the others were equally as curious as Evan was.

Evan rose to his feet and quickly asked, "What is it? What's wrong?"

Rachel answered excitedly. "We need to leave. My unit has been called up, and we are being sent to New Orleans to help clean up Hurricane Katrina."

Rachel's mom chimed in. "I've seen a lot of that damage on TV, and it's awful. You be careful down there."

"I'll be fine," replied Rachel confidently. She gathered her things and continued speaking to the group. "We leave the fort at 7:00 AM tomorrow, so I've got a lot to do."

"Tomorrow?" asked Evan. "Nice of them to give you at least a few hours notice. That's unbelievable."

"I know," echoed Rachel. "Evidently Louisiana just requested us, and they want us to get down there as soon as we can. I'm sorry everyone, but we have to go."

She gave quick hugs to everyone, and she and Evan sped home. The rest of her day was spent frantically packing her gear and planning at least a month's worth of lessons for her students. She called her principal, Mr. Allen, and filled him in on her orders. "I have no idea exactly how long I'll be gone, but I'll keep you posted. I'm sorry to do this to you with such short notice, but I just found out a couple hours ago myself."

"It's fine," responded Mr. Allen. "We'll get your classes covered and try to stay with the lesson plans you leave. Evan can just bring them up to me in the morning. We're proud of your service."

"Thank you," beamed Rachel. "I'll see you when I get back."

Mr. Allen had no idea how many times he would get similar phone calls from Rachel in the months ahead.

Since her unit was leaving very early the next morning, Rachel thought it would be better to leave for the fort that night and already be there when she woke up, rather than chancing an unforeseen problem in the morning that could make her late. Evan helped her load her vehicle and by 8:00 that evening she was ready to go. They stood in their driveway wrapped together in a long hug, one that would have to last at least a month. She looked at her watch, and they both knew she had to leave. Rachel finally made it official. "I have to go," she whispered.

"I know. I'll echo your mom though. Be careful."

She smiled and laughed. "Don't worry. Wherever the army takes me, I'll always come back to you. This is why I joined the Guard." Following a long, romantic kiss, Rachel climbed into her car and drove away.

Evan stood motionless in the driveway as she turned the corner and disappeared from his view, and then he sat on the front step for several minutes, trying to imagine what lay ahead for his wife. Rachel had been a soldier in the National Guard when Evan first met her, and for him, it was an appealing part of who she was. He had always been proud of her service, and he gladly shared her with her unit one weekend every month. This, however, was different. He wondered to himself how this experience would change her. She would surely be thrown into scenes of destruction and death, and those things can change everyone.

Evan had one more beer following his sidewalk café meal, and he sat and watched the nameless people continue to pass by him. While he watched, he remembered that month when Rachel had been gone. He remembered the stories she had told him when she had returned home, stories of the great horrors she had seen. There had been many, and he remembered being somewhat uncomfortable by the enthusiasm she had shown each time she had recounted her adventures.

She had even temporarily lost her sense of smell on that trip, and Evan couldn't imagine a stench potent or constant enough to do that to a person in such a short time, but something had caused it. Her vocabulary changed too. Evan had already seen an increase in her swearing and rough talk just from drill weekends, but this was way beyond that. It got to the point where Evan had to ask her to clean up her words. He remembered the surprise in Rachel's face, as she wasn't even aware of how she had been talking. He often wondered to himself what kinds of conversations could so rapidly change her words so dramatically, yet those words rolled out of her mouth with such ease that it seemed to be natural for her. At times, her language was so rough that Evan had to look and make sure that it was really Rachel who was speaking.

Evan remembered one other very odd day after she got back from New Orleans when Rachel decided that she wanted to bake something. He wasn't sure what was in the oven, but after a while, she was off doing something in another part of the house, and he knew he could smell something burning. The aroma was potent, and Evan knew something was very wrong. He quickly rushed into the kitchen and saw smoke billowing from their oven. "Holy cow!" he exclaimed. "What happened here? Rachel get in here!" He turned the oven off, opened the door, and the smoke filled the kitchen. The burned smell began to get the best of him, and he began coughing.

Rachel came in and was horrified as she saw the results of her cooking project. She fought through the smoke, grabbed hot-pan holders, and brought the tray out of the oven. She dropped the smoldering pan into the sink and opened several windows to help alleviate the smoke in the room. Whatever she had intended on baking had turned into black globs that smelled as bad as they looked.

"Did you forget you were cooking?" he asked. "That smell is awful."

"I got busy with my computer stuff and lost track of how long it had been in the oven," she answered.

"Couldn't you smell it? It made me sick from where I was sitting in the living room."

Rachel paused for a second and then walked to the sink. She slightly bent over and then gave Evan an odd look. "I can't smell anything even this close. That's weird. I can't smell it at all."

"That's unbelievable," responded Evan. "Right now I wish I couldn't smell anything either. It's terrible. Man, how potent were the odors in New Orleans if it killed your sense of smell in just a month?"

"It was pretty bad, but I just thought I had gotten used to it. I guess not. There was stagnant standing water everywhere, and we weren't allowed to even step in it. The stench was pretty incredible."

"I can't even imagine. Do you need help cleaning this up?"

"No, I've got it," she answered. The smoke in the kitchen had begun to clear, but the odor continued to hang over the entire house. Evan again wondered to himself about her month away from him. He wondered about all the things she had really seen and done, and he was not anxious to find out what other effects of that trip would be revealed to him in the days ahead.

CHAPTER 3

E van rose from the restaurant table, left a large tip, and began walking again. He walked without any real purpose toward an unknown destination. Maybe escaping by himself wasn't the best answer for Evan, but he had felt like a prisoner at home, and he knew he had to leave, at least for a while. He had been an optimist for as much of his life as he could remember, and somewhere inside himself, he was searching for the silver lining in his current situation. The afternoon wasn't quite ready to surrender to the evening yet, so Evan hopped into his rented convertible and drove. With the top down, the warm breeze caressed his face as he left Fort Myers and crossed the bridge to Sanibel Island. The scene before him looked like a watercolor painting of paradise. Beautiful long stretches of blue water surrounded the bridge and dominated the foreground of the canvas. The outlines of trees, beach houses, and sailboats filled the middle of the painting, and the picture was completed by the cloudless blue winter sky above. Had he really been shoveling snow yesterday at home?

Evan stopped at the toll booth and paid the six dollars required to drive onto the island. When he drove through the toll gate, he knew he had entered an entirely new world, a world connected to the mainland but very much full of its own unique individuality. He drove down the main highway that ran the length of the island, gazing at the shops, restaurants, homes, and endless palm trees. He had seen them once before, but everything was new again. At the north end of the island, he found a public beach and decided to see what it had to offer him. He frowned when he paid the five dollars to park his car, but he paid it and then walked leisurely toward the sand.

This beach was far rougher than Fort Myers Beach and was far more deserted, which was fine with Evan. The laughter, fun, and play he had watched at the other beach didn't seem to match his mood, but this one did. The cool wind, the whitecaps, and the mostly deserted stretches of sand suited him much better. He knew that here he could walk without distraction or just sit and try and sort out the myriad of thoughts and emotions that plagued him. He could even let out that scream he had thought of earlier if he so desired. He chose to sit in the sand and attempt to drink in his tropical surroundings.

Eventually, the sun began fading in the distance, and Evan was surprised how quickly the temperature began to fall. The gulf breeze now felt cold on his sunburned legs and shoulders, and he wished he had brought along pants and a jacket. He realized that his shorts and T-shirt were clearly now not enough to keep him warm, yet the sea mesmerized him for another half hour until he realized that he was shivering uncontrollably.

There were two couples walking hand in hand on the beach as Evan quickly made his way back to his convertible. He was jealous of them immediately, and their cheerful smiles and shared warmth served as a visual contrast to Evan's solitary shivering. He put the top back up on his car and even turned the heater on for a few moments to get rid of the chill he felt. He quickly warmed up again and as he recrossed the bridge to the mainland and returned to Fort Myers he became frustrated that the more desolate beach hadn't really helped him sort anything out. He wondered if there was any place that could do that.

Back in his hotel room, Evan grabbed a beer from his room's refrigerator and pulled a chair out onto his deck. The traffic moved along below him, totally unaware of and not caring about the solitary figure watching them from above. Nobody at all knew him there, and for now, that was how Evan wanted it. He wanted to be anonymous and invisible as he tried to sort his life out. He thought back to the ending of the movie *City Slickers,* and he wondered if his life could be a "do over" like one of the characters' life was. Can a person change everything in his life and remake himself at fifty? He had already done that four years earlier with Rachel, and he wondered if he had the strength to do it again now without her. He knew that in general, people resist major changes in their lives and much prefer existing in their comfort zones. Evan didn't mind change and often sought it out, but he enjoyed change on his terms. This time he felt like change was being forced upon him whether he wanted it or not, and that made him angry.

Three months after returning from New Orleans, Rachel had come to Evan with more news. They had been sitting in the living room, and during a commercial break in the show they were watching, she began, "I have a chance to go to Panama for two or three weeks. A colonel at the fort wants me to go with him and I told him I wanted to go."

Evan was caught a bit off guard. "Panama? What will you be doing there?"

"I think I'll be translating for him. He's got to do something with some government officials there, and he doesn't speak Spanish. It's a great chance to put my Spanish degree to work, see some more of the world, and get paid to do it."

"When do you leave?" inquired Evan, who now sat fully upright in his chair.

"Not sure but it's pretty soon," responded Rachel. "The colonel told me he would let me know in the next day or two."

Evan smiled and tried to share her enthusiasm for the trip. "This didn't just happen. How long have you known about all this?"

She spoke more quietly after that question. "About a week."

"You've known for a week and didn't say anything to me about it?" His previous enthusiasm left immediately. "Why would it take you that long to tell me?"

She was momentarily at a loss. "I don't know. I guess I was just waiting for the right moment and waiting to see if it actually became official."

"I think you're starting to like official things more every day, aren't you?" Evan just shook his head. He couldn't help but feel that things between Rachel and him were changing, and he was more right than he could have ever imagined.

"What do you mean I like 'official'?" she asked.

"Well, I thought we always shared things like that, not kept them secret. Suddenly the only things that seem to hold your interest are military things and your next adventures."

"Sorry," she answered. "This can be a really good thing for me."

"I'm sure that's true. What comes after that and after that? Are you working on being gone all the time? How good is all that for us?"

"We'll be fine. You know that's one of the reasons I joined the Guard."

"Yeah, I know."

Two weeks following her announcement, Rachel was again packed and gone, this time for Panama. She was part of a diplomatic group that spent three weeks coordinating activities between Panama and the United States, and she was front and center relaying and translating important conversations for powerful people. Evan understood completely why she had been so eager to go. She had an important role to play with this group, and for the most part, he was very proud of her.

The start of her second week in Panama marked another landmark day though it passed much more quietly than Evan had wanted it to. Evan and Rachel's first anniversary arrived, and despite some elaborate romantic plans, Evan had to settle for a romantic e-mail message. He had planned a real date night, complete with a movie and a dinner at Rachel's favorite restaurant, but those plans had to be scrapped because she was out of the country. He had thought ahead before she left though and had secretly placed an anniversary card in her luggage so she would find it when she arrived in Panama. He enjoyed doing creative, surprising things like that because he knew Rachel had never had anyone do things like that for her, and he knew that even though she enjoyed acting tough and strong most of the time, she appreciated his efforts in making her feel loved and wanted and feminine. It was their first anniversary, a very special day, and he had been deprived of fully getting to enjoy it and share it with his wife.

Rachel returned two weeks after their anniversary, full of excitement and energy. Before she had even unpacked her bags, she began telling Evan about her trip. "It was a blast. The colonel told me he would be making future trips down there, and he was so impressed with me that he wants me to go with him again."

Evan knew that she would have left the following day if given the chance, yet he forced a smile and replied, "That's great. I'm proud of you. Your Spanish must have been very good."

"I guess it was good enough."

It was déjà vu for Evan as he sat and listened to Rachel's travel stories though she seemed to have a lot more to tell him than she had when she had returned from New Orleans. This time he heard about her time in Miami changing planes, the long flight over the Caribbean Sea, a full day at the Panama Canal, and three weeks at a luxury hotel. Many other tales poured from Rachel's memory as he sat and listened. He didn't have much to add to the conversation, so he just listened and asked a few questions as she continued retelling her adventures. His three weeks at home had been mundane in comparison, including the hamburger he had cooked for himself on their anniversary night.

To Evan's disappointment, Rachel never mentioned their anniversary as she recounted her trip, but he did ask her if she had found the card he had hidden in her luggage.

"Yes, I did," she smiled. "Thanks. It was very nice. We'll make up for it next year on our anniversary, okay?"

"Deal," agreed Evan.

Rachel immediately jumped back into her teaching job, but Evan could see some real changes. Her attitude, her effort, her patience level, and her demeanor were all different than they had been. Her free-time hours were now spent on military things instead of teaching projects. Hours of research on promotion possibilities were combined with calls and e-mails filled with inquiries regarding possible travel to other countries. Something had been ignited inside her with her two trips, and Evan wondered how far she truly desired to take that. Was he now married to a soldier instead of a teacher? Was she happier when she was in uniform and gone to some other place than she was at home with him? How could he even ask her such a question, especially when he wasn't sure he really wanted to know the answer? The changes in her didn't worry him yet because her enthusiasm was contagious, but the potential for her travels to continue and become far more frequent nagged at Evan far more than he cared to admit. One of Evan's joys at home was cooking their evening meal and sitting at the table with Rachel to talk and enjoy whatever he had fixed for them, but apparently, her eating habits had changed, and those meals and conversations didn't happen much after her return from Panama, so he found himself cooking a lot of hamburgers for one.

CHAPTER 4

Evan finished his beer on the hotel deck and went back to his room. He would have liked to have gotten a seaside room, but those cost more and were booked far in advance. This had been a spur-of-the-moment weekend trip, so he resigned himself to watching cars from his balcony instead of watching waves. He was now hungry again and wished he had stopped somewhere and gotten some snacks to eat in his room.

He decided to go out and eat and was glad that even the fancy restaurants along the beach didn't have stuffy dress codes. The nicest he could wear with what he had packed was a pair of jeans, a polo shirt, and tennis shoes. He had remembered seeing an Italian place not far away, and he decided that he would give it a try. He never enjoyed sitting alone in a restaurant and eating a meal, but he understood that eating alone most of the time was now his reality and his world. The Italian restaurant was very cozy, and Evan was shown to a small table that faced the highway. The checkerboard tablecloths added greatly to the atmosphere, and Italian music played softly in the background. The room was filled with families and couples, and Evan suddenly felt isolated and out of place. He thought for a moment about getting up and walking out, but hunger defeated his other emotions, and he stayed and tried to enjoy his meal.

He could overhear conversations from nearby tables as couples discussed their futures, talking about how wonderful it would be to retire in a place like Fort Myers. Evan and Rachel had once shared similar dreams of a warm-weather island life, free from cold and snow and most responsibility. Evan sarcastically smiled at the couple, raised his wine glass, and silently toasted romantic naivety. He had been there recently too, yet he also secretly hoped all the plans he heard them making came true for them.

The plans had sounded so appealing to both Evan and Rachel. It was interesting to Evan how the dream had gone from something totally abstract to far more detailed and tangible over time. When Rachel returned from Panama, the plans got even more real. She had even gone as far as pricing land and homes while she was there, filing the information away for someday. Looking back, Evan realized that Rachel's plans and dreams changed easily and often, based on her immediate situation and surroundings. She was full of plans that would never come to pass, but he knew that part of her believed they would actually happen. As a spouse, he had a choice to make. He could either encourage those dreams no matter what or he could kill them. That was an easy decision.

Evan had seen this, beginning with their honeymoon, and it had seemed innocent and fun, so he gladly went along with everything. Seeing the endless ways tourists were willing to spend their money, Rachel's mind raced with plans and ideas. Before the honeymoon week was over, she had at least four specific money-making propositions they could get into if they ever moved to Myrtle Beach permanently. Evan was open-minded enough to see the possibilities as well, but he was quite content with the life they had just begun and with where they currently lived, so he didn't get too serious about any of the plans, but he agreed to also file them away for someday. When Evan heard Rachel talk about buying land and a house in Panama, he thought back to their honeymoon, and he wondered if Rachel's thoughts were really that easily swayed by her surroundings. Once the Panama retirement options entered the picture, the beach-life, tourist-trap ideas for South Carolina were never discussed again.

Evan paid his food bill, complimented the waitress, tipped her well, and made his way to the door. The sunshine of the day was gone and had been replaced with the eye-catching neon that embraced the Florida night life. He had no real desire to return to his hotel room so that he could sit alone for the rest of the night, and he looked down the highway for an alternative. He looked to the west and saw the enticing lights of a nightclub, and the steady stream of people entering the building helped make up his mind. Evan entered the Sand Crabbe with no expectations other than hoping it was a good place to kill a few hours. He thought perhaps he could summon a reason to end his day with a smile of some kind.

The band was rocking from the stage, and all the tables were full as Evan wedged his way through the crowd and found one of the few available stools at the bar. The tropical decor was warm and inviting. The walls were covered with paintings and drawings of waves and sea creatures that were just the thing for any northern tourist to be happily reminded that, at least for a while, he wasn't at home. He fully surveyed the room and was a bit jealous of so many people able to relax, laugh, and cut loose. He knew that each person there had a unique story just as he did, and he couldn't help but wonder how many in the club were simply pretending to act happy. Before long, the bartender made his way to Evan, and Evan decided to start with a beer. The music was a mix or rock and reggae, and the band's skill and energy had the place jumping. The dance floor overflowed, and Evan found himself tapping his toes to the music. When the band began their rendition of "Cheeseburger in Paradise," Evan began to laugh. The irony got the best of him as he thought again about his solitary first-anniversary meal, and he contrasted that image with the beach setting where he now found himself.

Evan's laughter got the attention of the man sitting to his left, and the two struck up a conversation. The man was in his forties and looked athletic. His face was serious yet friendly, and it was obvious his hands were no stranger to physical labor. He told Evan that he was down from Minnesota, escaping the cold for a week. His wife had taken their children to a movie, and he had decided to check out the Sand Crabbe while they were gone. Evan found out that the man was also in the military and had done two tours in Iraq. His most recent tour had been completed just five months earlier.

That fact piqued Evan's interest greatly, and he bought Tony, his new friend, a drink and asked if he could quiz him a bit about his tours and his family. Tony was naturally a talker and said that he would be happy to tell his story if Evan really wanted to hear it. He did.

Evan began. "Fort Myers is a lot nicer than a Minnesota December, isn't it?"

Tony grinned largely. "Oh yeah. No comparison. It's an easy trade for me giving up ice for warm beaches."

"I hear that," responded Evan. "I did the same and can't believe how nice it is here. There are some things I'd really like to pick your brain on regarding your Iraq tours, and if I get too personal, just tell me, okay?"

"Ask away. If I can answer you, I'll sure do it." Tony took a long sip of his beer and waited for Evan's first question.

"All right," stated Evan, who suddenly wore a more serious look on his face. "Was there a big difference between your first year and your second year away from home?"

Tony again grinned. "Excellent question, my friend. I can already tell you're serious about this discussion. There was a huge difference between the two tours for both my family and me. My first year over there was almost surreal and dreamlike. It was just a year, and from the day I got there, the end was in sight, so both my wife and I looked at the deployment as a temporary inconvenience and a chance for me to serve proudly.

"My friends and family were completely supportive and helpful, and I had the Internet to communicate often with my family. I was like a celebrity in our little Minnesota town, and for that whole first year, my wife and kids got some of the same kind of celebrity treatment too."

Evan listened intently. "That sounds familiar. What about your time at home in between tours?"

"When I got home, I was even more of a celebrity as I told all my stories, and life was generally pretty good. I just went back to being a husband, dad, friend, and employee. After a while, Iraq was no longer a daily topic of discussion with my friends, and for five months, I just lived my normal routine."

"And then?" interjected Evan.

"And then everything changed," replied Tony more solemnly, squirming a bit on his stool. "The excitement of my first tour was replaced with a form of dread for the second one. Family plans were again forced to be put on hold. I had to ask my boss for another extended leave of absence to keep my job, and my wife was again going to have to be both the man and woman of the house."

"So it was pretty much instantly a negative for your whole family when you got your orders for your second tour," surmised Evan. "I really appreciate you sharing all this with me. I knew there had to be a lot of other people whose lives changed a lot because of deployments, but I've never gotten to really talk about it with anyone."

"I'm happy to talk about it. Don't know if it will help you any, but I can tell you how it was for me. It definitely was a negative getting ready for my second tour. My wife and I hated the thought of another year lost from our marriage, sleeping alone, missing out on the touches, the closeness, and of course, the romance. I also saw it as another year forever lost watching my kids grow up and mature. None of us was happy about my going back a second time."

Tony bought the next round as the two continued their talk with "Margaritaville" playing in the background. The comfort level between the two continued to rise, and Evan enjoyed having an outlet to ask real questions and to share previously hidden feelings without any fear of being judged.

"Did you and your wife go anywhere or do anything special during your two-week leave?"

A broad knowing grin appeared on Tony's face. "You've been there, haven't you? Lots of people have asked me about my tours and the things I saw and did over there, but you're the first one to ever ask me about these kinds of things and the mental toll two years apart can have on a marriage and a family."

Evan returned the smile and softly added, "Yeah, I've been there, and it wasn't good."

"I flew home from Iraq after the mandatory stop in Kuwait, and I spent the first three days getting to know my children again. It took me that long to recover from the jet lag and get my body on Minnesota time."

"I can't even imagine how tiring those twenty-hour flights must be."

"There's nothing like it. All I did was sit and I was exhausted." Tony shook his head as he remembered the long flights. "Don't ever want to do that again."

"So you just stayed at home the whole time?"

"Oh no. The fourth day, my wife and I flew to Fort Lauderdale and got on a cruise ship. We both thought a cruise would be a great way for us to enjoy some of our short time together while I was back."

"I'm jealous," sighed Evan. "I've always wanted to do that." On the surface, a cruise seemed romantic and perfect, but Evan knew very well that appearances were rarely, if ever, the entire story, and he continued his questions. "So it was wonderful?" Tony then began reliving his eight days at sea, remembering each port he and his wife had visited. "It was great. We toured an old fort in San Juan, Puerto Rico, and rode in a glass-bottom submarine on St. Thomas. We spent an awesome day at a hidden lagoon on Tortola and walked around Antigua for most of a day. Our last stop was Nassau, and we took a water taxi to the Atlantis. That place is unbelievable!"

"I've seen pictures and it looks very impressive," commented Evan.

"Our cabin on the ship was filled with hats, shirts, and all kinds of souvenirs, and it was a big challenge packing all the stuff just to get off the boat. If I ever go again, I'm bringing an extra empty suitcase just for the things I know I'll buy on the trip."

They both chuckled at human nature and our desire for mementos and reminders of our life experiences. Evan liked souvenirs too, so he could understand Tony's packing dilemma after visiting five exotic places.

"How about the days at sea in between ports? What did you do?" Evan continued.

"Those were fun too. We plopped our butts onto the deck chairs and tanned and read and talked. I spent as much time as I could sampling all the buffets, and of course, I donated my share to the ship's casino." He paused there for a second. "Those slots are pretty tight."

"I've heard that," laughed Evan, "but I'm sure I'd play them too if I went on a cruise. It sounds like the cruise was a great decision for you and your wife to reconnect. I'm glad for you."

"Well, the days were a lot of fun," continued Tony, "but after every day, there is a night. I don't really want to go too far into that. Let's just say it was a lot easier being tourist buddies than it was being romantic spouses."

Evan gave an understanding nod. "Enough said."

"Thanks. I've never talked about this stuff with anyone. Fate is a funny thing, isn't it? Of all the days of the year and all the bars in town, you and I ended up sitting side by side. I'm glad."

"Me too," chimed Evan as the two tapped their beer glasses together, cementing a bond of shared experiences. They finished their beers and ordered more as the band played Jimmy Buffet's "Come Monday." Neither man wanted to think about Monday.

The next hour was spent with much lighter conversation, covering topics that ranged from snow and sports to beaches and bikinis. The dance floor was still full, and whether it was the music or the conversation or a combination of the two, Evan had found his smile.

Tony looked at his watch and knew that the movie had finished. His family was probably back at their hotel, and he knew he should join them there. The two men exchanged cell phone numbers, and Evan knew he had a friendly shoulder to lean on in the future if needed. They shook hands, and Tony fought through the crowd of partiers, heading back to rejoin his family. Evan watched him until he disappeared into the crowd and then Evan turned his attention back to the band, alone again but not quite as alone as before.

CHAPTER 5

The inevitable end of the night arrived, and Evan unwillingly left the bar and slowly drove back to his hotel. He turned the key to his room door, and once inside, he immediately turned on the television to remove the silence. Bedtime had turned into Evan's least favorite time of every single day. He had become a master of making himself so tired at night that he would usually fall asleep quickly, but even that didn't always work. It was lying in bed when Evan felt the most alone, and far too often for his own comfort, his mind would wander to the past. When that happened, sleep became nearly impossible for him, and his stress level rose dramatically. He hated the solitary nights more than anything else. The promise had been so different. The promise had been shared nights that followed shared days for a lifetime. Where had it all gone so wrong?

Evan undressed and climbed into bed as Jimmy Stewart was going hoarse on the Senate floor in *Mr. Smith Goes to Washington*. The combination of the beer, the movie, and the late hour worked as a sedative, and Evan fell asleep quickly without having to endure any of the near-sleep thinking time that had haunted him so often in recent days.

He woke six hours later to the morning weatherman predicting a warm, perfect Saturday. Evan rubbed his eyes and tried to focus on the television screen. The sun was already shining brightly and poured into his room through the large windows. He watched some of the morning news with no real interest and then made his way to the shower. When the warm water hit his shoulders, he was quickly reminded of the sun he got the day before, but he was determined to add to his sunburn today regardless. He knew the sting would only be temporary, and when he returned to the snow and cold, he would have a tan with which he could taunt his friends.

Evan poured himself a cup of coffee and made his way to his deck to greet the Florida morning. Last night had been extremely helpful to him. He felt as if he had regained some balance in his thinking, and when a person was struggling with his thoughts, it was comforting to find another person who had been through similar tests and difficulties. He raised his coffee cup and silently thanked destiny for placing Tony in his path. He hoped with all his heart that Tony felt better too and that he and his family would have a successful and happy future. In the background, he heard the television announcer give a quick rundown of local birthdays, and as he looked over the railing at the morning weekend beach traffic, he thought back to his birthday four years earlier. That day should have been a sign for him, but he hadn't seen it. He wondered how many other signs he had missed along the way.

Evan had always tried very hard to come up with something creative to mark special days with Rachel. He had done something special for each of her birthdays, the anniversary of their first date, Christmas, and so on. He enjoyed doing those things for her even if she was sometimes unsure of how to show her appreciation. He knew that she had never had anyone truly love her just for who she was, and perhaps that was why she was always trying to prove herself. Rachel possessed many wonderful qualities that had attracted Evan, but her belief that she always had to prove she was tougher and stronger than others had never appealed to him.

Evan's birthday had arrived without fanfare. Like other forty-five-year-olds, he didn't need a big fuss made over the event, but he didn't turn down a little special attention from those closest to him either. He assumed that Rachel had something special planned for him since it was his first birthday since they had gotten married. Her birthday had been two months earlier, and Evan had made the day as memorable and special for her as he could.

By midafternoon on that day, Evan thought Rachel was just being coy. He remembered everything vividly. She hadn't mentioned anything at all about his birthday, and by then, he wasn't about to. He decided to let his anticipation build until she was ready to unveil whatever her surprise might have been, but when bedtime arrived, all of Evan's good feelings had vanished and had been replaced with disappointment, sadness, and frustration. There had been nothing from her. No card, no gift, no mention or acknowledgment at all, and he finally decided to vent a bit before his day ended. Rachel was in the recliner in their living room, reading a novel, and Evan stood across the room and said, "I'm going to bed."

She momentarily looked up from her book and answered, "Good night. I'm going to read a while longer."

Instead of walking toward their bedroom, he stood frozen and gave her a hard look. She was already back in the world of her novel when he spoke again. "You know it would have been nice to at least hear 'happy birthday' from you once today."

The reading instantly stopped, and Rachel wore a look of horror on her face. "Why would I tell you that today when your birthday is still two days away?"

Her question brought out a sarcastic laugh from Evan. "I'm pretty sure I know when my birthday is. I figured you knew when it was too, but I guess you don't."

"Oh my gawd, are you serious? It's today?" she shrieked. "I could have sworn it was in two days. I feel horrible."

"Really. Try and guess how I feel. Enjoy your book." With that, he turned and walked an angry and disappointed walk toward the bedroom, knowing full well he had left her sitting speechless in the recliner. For the next two days, Rachel tried to make amends for forgetting his birthday, but what was done was done and, for Evan, could not be totally fixed. As the Fort Myers TV announcer continued to talk, Evan knew he should have paid more attention to times like that.

After his coffee, he decided to take a morning stroll on the beach. It was low tide, and the beach looked completely different than when he had been there the day before. The sand stretched further out into the Gulf, and it was littered with far more shells than it had been when he had first seen it. It was another reminder to him of how even major things could evolve and change in a short period of time. For the two years he and Rachel had dated, her military time away from him had been limited to her one weekend a month and her two weeks of camp in the summer. Apparently, she had always been quietly working on ways to do more military things and take more trips because after her month in New Orleans and her two trips to Panama, the floodgates opened.

The first summer they were married, Rachel found two different two-week military training schools to attend besides her summer camp. Evan was spending more and more time alone, but Rachel had convinced him that all these trips would lead to promotions for her and a better future for them, so he supported what she wanted to do.

Other than Rachel forgetting Evan's birthday, the rest of their first autumn together was mostly smooth and uneventful. Thanksgiving was spent with Evan's family, and Christmas was enjoyed with Rachel's family. The two groups lived five hundred miles apart, and the couple knew it wasn't feasible to try and be in both places each holiday. That arrangement seemed to suit everyone on both sides of the family. On Christmas afternoon, Evan and Rachel each drove to her brother's house. Rachel usually liked to stay longer and visit with her mom, so taking two cars seemed to make sense. By early evening, everyone was sitting lazily in the living room. Gifts had been exchanged and opened and were now being enjoyed. The first meal had been eaten, and the adults were sitting in the living room, watching the kids play with their new games and toys. Most of the adults were contemplating naps when the lightning struck.

Rachel, out of the blue, announced to the room, "I won't be seeing any of you again for a while. In three weeks or so, I'll be leaving for Guatemala, and I'll be working with a construction detail there." Evan remembered how casually she had dropped her bomb on the room.

The news seemed to perk everyone in the room up, and any thought of naps was quickly forgotten. Her mom was the first to respond to her. "Guatemala? How long will you be there?"

"Not sure, but it looks like five or six months. It's a huge project."

Her mom smiled, "My daughter, the globe-trotter."

"That's me!" exclaimed Rachel excitedly.

Across the room, Evan sat quietly, wearing a look of disbelief on his face. His eyes met Rachel's, and there could be little doubt in her mind what he was thinking and feeling. "You leave in three weeks and will be gone for five or six months? Good grief! How long have you known about this?" he asked her sharply.

Rachel answered with a less enthusiastic tone than before. "It just became official, but it's been in the works for a while."

Evan stood up and spoke very sarcastically. "Ah, yes, the official things again. That's just great." Tension suddenly filled the room as he left to find his coat. He returned and looked at Rachel's mom. "Thanks for the meal, but I think I'll go home now. Merry Christmas, everyone."

He then turned to Rachel and was silently glad they had each driven there in separate vehicles. "I can't believe you don't tell me stuff like this until you're almost ready to leave. Do you really think it only affects you?"

Rachel looked at him blankly. "I thought you'd be excited too."

He looked her straight in the eyes. "Right. See me jumping up and down and doing cartwheels? Good-bye, everyone."

Evan started his car and immediately tore out of the driveway. It was twenty-five miles back home, and he got angrier with each mile he drove. It seemed more like Halloween to him than Christmas, and he felt like the victim of a cruel trick-or-treat prank. He couldn't believe she had just announced that in three short weeks she would leave him again and this time for five or six months. She had never mentioned anything about this, had given him no clue at all. Evan had come to know enough about the military and its planning to know that no project this large was planned and organized on short notice. She must have known she was leaving for at least two months, if not longer. His frustration grew, and he didn't care when or if Rachel made it home that night. He wasn't sure he'd be able to put his emotions into words, but he knew he'd soon have to. A potentially unpleasant conversation was on the near horizon.

Four hours later, Rachel's car pulled into their driveway, and she walked to the house with her arms full of Christmas gifts she had received. Once inside, she set the gifts down and took a seat on the couch. Evan was in the recliner and had not spoken when she came in.

"I can't believe you just walked out like that," she began. "It was embarrassing."

Evan sat up in the recliner and rested his elbows on his knees. "You can't? You really can't? How could you think that you suddenly being gone for half a year would excite me?"

"You know that seeing the world is something I really want to do, and that's the main reason I joined the Guard. Now I'm getting that chance, and I thought you'd be a little more supportive."

"Don't you think that my level of support might have been a little bit higher if you hadn't sprung it on me at the same time you told everyone else?"

"Probably so, but it wasn't official yet."

"So in your mind, you're only going to share things with me when they are official? That's ridiculous."

"That's not what I meant," she answered defiantly.

"Maybe, maybe not, but that's what you did, and I don't like it. How could I be excited about half a year here alone? I was alone before we got married, and I thought I was all done with that."

"That's not fair."

"Of course it's fair. It's what I'm feeling. Look ahead a little ways at those next five months. You'll be out of the country for both of our first two anniversaries. How happy should that make me? And what comes after this trip? Are you only happy now when you are somewhere else?"

"Anniversaries can be celebrated at other times if need be, can't they?" she asked.

"I guess with us they have to be," replied Evan fairly sarcastically.

With that, the conversation was over. Rachel went into the kitchen, and Evan returned to his movie, *It's a Wonderful Life*. George Bailey was just telling his guardian angel, Clarence, that it probably would have been better if he had never been born.

CHAPTER 6

The beach was far more empty than it would be a few hours later, and Evan enjoyed the peaceful morning sounds of the waves splashing onto the shore. He found it ironic that he had spent over two years hating solitude, yet here, for now, it appealed to him. He quickly understood the difference, however. This time, the solitude was his choice. Even though the water was cold, Evan removed his sandals and carried them. He walked along in the ankle-deep water watching freighters in the distance, wondering to himself where they were headed. He thought he could see a cruise ship far off on the horizon and guessed that it was headed to Key West. He thought of Tony and his wife and their cruise trip and again silently hoped everything would work out well for them.

The weatherman on television had been right. The temperature was rising quickly, and Evan could not spot any clouds in the sky. Steady streams of people were placing their towels on the sand, setting up chairs, and claiming their spots on the beach for a day of fun and sun. Evan grinned as he watched the eager children run into the water and then run back out just as quickly once they realized the water was far colder than they had hoped or imagined.

Evan was glad that he was at least able to smile again. It had seemed like a foreign thing to him at first, but he was becoming more at ease with trying to be somewhat happy again. He had come to realize that while he had some pretty major things yet to sort out, it wasn't going to hurt him to try and enjoy the days he would still be living.

He tossed some dead sand dollars back into the Gulf and walked the beach a while longer. Every time he thought back to Rachel's Christmas bombshell announcement, he fumed, even now, all this time later, when it no longer mattered at all. In all the time the two had been together, they had never had a real sustained argument. In fact, the two nearly always saw things with the same eyes and, up until that Christmas moment, had always discussed and planned major future plans together. The dreams had always been shared because they both believed those dreams could only be reached as a team, and Evan had greatly resented not being included at all with a decision that would dramatically change his world for at least five or six months. Nearly four years after the fact, he had to admit to himself that he had been totally stunned that Christmas afternoon.

Had she really thought that she was the only one her decision affected? How could she just pick up and leave him so easily for such a long time? Was he supposed to be excited for her adventure and just tolerate his half a year alone without her? Their first and second anniversaries spent in separate countries were not what he had signed on for. He had been alone long enough prior to meeting Rachel, and he thought he would never have to deal with that again once he found her. He had been under the impression that marriage meant that two people were actually together. He reached down and picked up another sand dollar and threw it as far out into the water as he could.

The three weeks between Christmas and Rachel's leaving day were very cool. Conversation between the two was minimal and generally superficial. Romance and touching were both absent, despite the fact the two would be away from each other for a very long time, and the lack of touching and closeness made for a few incredibly awkward weeks. Rachel spent her time lining up nearly a semester's worth of work and activities for her students, who would now spend almost half a school year in the hands of a substitute teacher. The remainder of her limited

time was spent between spending time with her mom and packing all
the things she could fit into her military trunks. When it came time
for her to actually leave, her vehicle was stuffed full, and her excitement
level was sky-high. They both stood beside her car, knowing that the
moment for her to leave was again upon them. Evan ended the silence.
"Have you got everything?"

Rachel looked in her backseat and then in her trunk and calmly
answered, "I think so."

"And so it begins," continued Evan. "Be careful down there. You
have no idea what it will be like once you get there."

Rachel forced a smile. "I'll be fine and the time will pass quickly. I
should have Internet access most of the time, and I'll buy an international
cell phone once I get down there. We can communicate a lot."

"Okay," said Evan, trying his best to return the smile.

Evidently, Rachel could sense Evan's mood because she took his
hand. "Look, this is a great opportunity for me, and like I've always
told you, wherever I go in my uniform, I'll always come back to you.
You don't have to worry about that."

"I count on that," he replied. Then he kissed her good-bye and
opened the car door for her. She got in, smiled at him, and then she
was on her way.

For the third time, Evan watched his wife drive away from him
again on her way to another country. When he walked into their house,
the silence seemed very familiar to him. He knew it would be there,
but still it got his attention. Somehow it seemed more overwhelming
than the previous times, and this time, it was instant. Perhaps it was
the difference between being alone for three weeks versus knowing that
five empty months lay ahead. Walking the beach, it seemed interesting
to him that he was still able to see each of her leaving days so clearly in
his mind, even the ones from several years earlier.

He tossed a few more sand dollars into the water and then decided
to grab some breakfast. He thought an omelet and some bacon would
do him good, so he walked back to his hotel, brushed the sand off his

shoes, and got into his rental car. Prior to this trip, he had never driven a convertible before and really liked the novelty of driving along with the top down. He knew where he was headed for breakfast. He had seen it the night before, and as he drove, the thought of what he would soon be enjoying at IHOP started him salivating. Rachel loved a big breakfast at IHOP, and she had made Evan a believer as well. He could almost taste the pancakes and eggs and bacon as he pulled into the parking lot. The morning sun still bathed all of Fort Myers as Evan joined the throng of locals and snowbirds enjoying their meals. He was ushered to a booth and prepared to stuff himself with all he could eat.

Before his food arrived, Evan spied a morning newspaper that a previous diner had left. He grabbed it, brought it back to his seat, and checked out the news of the local area and the world. There were plenty of political stories and charts telling when the tide would change, and in the local section, a picture of a soldier caught his eye. There was a small story with the picture, and Evan began reading. The soldier in the picture was stationed in Iraq and had chosen to spend his two-week leave in the Fort Myers area. There was a group in town that had the sole purpose of lining up area businesses that were willing to give active-duty soldiers discounts and free deals on the services they offered. Many soldiers chose to spend time in the area, so the program had grown quite large.

Evan thought the program was a great idea, a wonderful way for a city to honor and give something back to those who served our country. This particular soldier was a sergeant from Illinois, and he had nothing but good things to say about the area and the program. He had taken advantage of some free golf, a haircut, and several free restaurant meals which the program offered to soldiers like him. The article of a soldier away from home once again took Evan's mind back to Rachel and her Guatemala trip.

The first five or six weeks she was gone were as she had said they would be. Evan got a lot of e-mails from her, each telling him about the things she was seeing and doing. It was obviously all new and exciting for her, just as Fort Myers had been for the Illinois soldier, and she was eager to share everything she was experiencing. Then something interesting happened, and everything changed.

Rachel had settled into a routine with her project, and things were no longer new there. Her work had become more automatic for her there as things do everywhere eventually, even in exotic places. Things at home were always routine for Evan. That rarely changed, so the e-mails between the two became shorter and more generic. Their anniversary also arrived once again, and again they were apart on that special day. Evan had again tucked a card deep inside Rachel's luggage with instructions that she should not open it until the day of their anniversary. She had done that and sent him an e-mail back, which puzzled him.

Happy anniversary to you too! Thanks for the card. It was hard not opening it until today but I resisted. Hope you had a great day.

Me

Looking back, Evan wondered if she would have even remembered the day without his card to remind her. At home, Evan celebrated his second anniversary the same way he had celebrated their first one the year before. He cooked himself a hamburger for supper and just spent the night feeling very alone.

The blueberry pancakes were incredibly good, and Evan ate them and the rest of his breakfast slowly because he was in no real hurry and had nowhere special to go. This trip was about thinking and reflecting, and the IHOP was as good as any other place for those things. He eventually finished reading the rest of the paper and reached the point where he couldn't eat another bite, so he paid his bill and strolled back into the warm Florida sunshine.

Evan started his car and decided just to drive. He had no plan and no real destination in mind but felt certain he would find something along the road to catch his interest. He turned south for no particular reason, eventually crossing the bridge that led away from Fort Myers Beach, and a few minutes later he found himself in Naples. He came to a stoplight at what was obviously a major intersection, and he decided to continue driving straight on the same road. Less than half a mile past the intersection, he saw a large structure off the road to his right, and the parking lot was full. The sign along the highway told him that the building was a dog track, so Evan quickly turned into the long driveway, and he knew he had found a place where he could think and play at the same time.

The races there didn't start for another hour, but there were many televisions already simulcasting horse races from several different racetracks. Evan found a table from where he could watch the action at three different tracks at once, and he settled in. He had ten minutes before the next race at Aqueduct, so he scanned the odds for each horse and decided on a 2-9 exacta. He placed a five-dollar bet and then returned to his table and ordered an iced tea from his waitress.

Even though the dogs weren't running yet, the outside doors to the track were open, and Evan went out to have a look. It was a simple track with no real frills, far less elaborate than others he had seen, but he knew very well that things didn't have to be fancy to be effective or good. In fact, that was how he tried to live his life in general. He liked to keep things as simple as possible, but like everyone else, he enjoyed nice things when he could have them. He was a guy who went through his closet a couple times a year and either gave away or threw away clothes he didn't wear anymore just to avoid any unnecessary clutter.

Rachel had bought into the concept of simplifying too. Neither liked clutter in their house and in their lives in general. Daily drama had been totally absent in their world, and that was by choice. As Evan looked over the manicured infield of the dog track, he realized he must have become a form of clutter in Rachel's mind. Her world had changed so dramatically because of the army that he viewed himself as comparable to an old shirt hanging unused for too long in her closet. What had surprised him the most was the ease with which she had been able to discard that shirt. He walked back inside in time to see that his exacta bet was not a winner, and he looked at the screen for the odds on each horse in the next race and decided to wait a while before placing his next bet.

CHAPTER 7

Spring had arrived, and the May flowers were in full bloom everywhere. Evan had to mow their lawn every week, but that was a chore he enjoyed. It was a fun diversion for him, and he liked the feelings of pride he felt when he finished, and the yard looked perfect. Rachel had been gone for four months, and life apart had become an unwanted daily reality for Evan.

Rachel surprised him one night with a rare phone call. After some general small talk, she got to the real substance of what she wanted to tell him.

"Some co-workers and I have earned some R & R, and we are heading to a beach resort on the coast for a week. We've got a bungalow rented there and get to kick back for a while."

"That sounds fun," added Evan. "I'm sure you'll have a good time."

"I wanted to make sure and let you know because I doubt I'll have any Internet service there, so I can't contact you."

"I appreciate that. I probably would have been wondering where you were for that long a time."

"That's what I figured, so I wanted to get you called before we left."

The rest of the call was the normal routine talk of her work, the weather, and the one or two things that had changed for Evan at home.

As she had predicted, there was no Internet service at the resort, so Evan had no contact with her while she was there. When she got back to her post following the vacation, however, he heard plenty, or more accurately, he read it in an e-mail.

> *Hi, the week was awesome and so was the resort! We had a full week of tanning, swimming, partying, and relaxing. It felt great! I've got some big news, I think. The place we stayed is actually for sale, and that got all our minds running in lots of directions. Property is cheap here, and we think we could make a go of it and make some real money if we bought it. We could have a residual income and a tropical place to retire. With four of us going in on it, we think we can make it work. I'll let you know more later.*

> *Me*

Evan read the e-mail and just shook his head. Wasn't it just ten short months ago that the plan was to buy a house in Panama and retire there? She hadn't discussed the first plan with him, but he had been open to it. Now it seemed to him that the Panamanian retirement plan was gone, and it had been replaced with a Guatemalan resort. The e-mail from Rachel was so full of enthusiasm that Evan thought this must be at least the start of a concrete plan. He wondered what kind of people his future business partners were, but if and when this plan became a reality, he knew he would meet them all eventually.

Evan made his way to the betting window and made his selections for the next race. He laughed to himself when he saw the name of the number 4 horse. R & R Paradise had to be a winner! He was an 18-1 long shot, but Evan combined him with two other horses that were among the favorites and placed a trifecta box bet. There were only two minutes until post time, so Evan returned to his seat and watched the television screen closest to him.

A Guatemalan resort. He shook his head and sighed because after the enthusiastic e-mail that day, he had never heard about that plan again. The same had been true regarding the house in Panama and the tourist-trap businesses in Myrtle Beach, and Evan mused silently that situational dreams were probably fine and very natural. They were certainly fun to think about even if they turned out to be nothing more than temporary pipe dreams.

He brought himself back to the moment at hand. The horses were in the starting gate, and the race got underway. Around the first turn, the favorites were biding their time in the middle of the pack, waiting for the right moment to turn on their speed. R & R Paradise was also in the middle of the pack. All three horses made their moves on the back stretch and came around the final turn neck and neck. Evan perked up and watched the stretch run intently. R & R Paradise actually pulled away from the others and won the race by two lengths, which surprised but greatly pleased Evan. Evan's other two horses came in second and third so Evan had won his trifecta bet. He waited eagerly for the winning amounts to be posted, and he knew he would like the result since his 18-1 horse had come in first.

A moment later, Evan let out a fairly loud cheer and even surprised himself. The numbers were posted, and he had won $345. It was the most emotion he had felt or shown in a long time, and he liked it. He walked with a grin and a purpose to the betting window to collect his winnings. He was enjoying himself partly because he had just won a large amount of money, but he also liked that he was anonymous in Naples, Florida. Nobody had a clue who he was, and that was very liberating to him. While Rachel had been gone, hardly a day had passed when he didn't get at least one question about where she was and how she was doing. Here he could enjoy his temporary invisibility, and that was what he did.

People began walking outside, and Evan realized that the dogs were about to begin running. He decided to join them, so he grabbed his tea and got a dog-racing program at the bar and then headed out into the beaming Florida sunshine. He chose a seat as close to the finish line as possible and began to look over the entries. He wondered if he could find another R & R Paradise long shot somewhere in the listings.

The woman sitting in front of Evan was busy with her cell phone. She told her husband that she had received some surprising news in an e-mail on her phone and was texting her reply. Evan raised his tea glass and knew he could relate to that kind of message. Just two short weeks after he had received the e-mail detailing Rachel's Guatemala resort trip, she had sent him another one that made his jaw drop and his heart sink. He could still remember the words of that e-mail.

The e-mail had begun with the normal pleasantries and then quickly shifted to the actual news.

> *Hi, hope all is well at home. It looks like our project here will be finished in about three weeks, and then I'll be coming back to the States. I'll need to go to Texas for at least a week first to square up the financial bookwork, and then I'll be heading home …*

That part of the e-mail made Evan smile. She was finally coming home to him. One short month and he and Rachel could again resume their life together and get to know each other one more time. He looked forward to that with both anticipation and anxiety. Five months apart was a long time, and he could only hope the two could find all the sparks that had burned so brightly for both of them not long ago. All those thoughts ended up being fleeting ones for Evan, for as he read more of the e-mail, a lump formed in his throat, and he forgot everything else he had been thinking. He would never forget the next few sentences no matter how long he lived.

> *My unit has been deployed to Iraq. They are already training to go, but since I'm here, I've been ordered to join them very soon after I I finish up with this trip. I'll only be home for two weeks then I report to Wisconsin to get ready for a year in Iraq. I'll tell you more soon.*

> *Me*

He knew the lady ahead of him in the bleachers texting her reply had nothing on him regarding surprise e-mails. He remembered being numb for several minutes after reading Rachel's words. It had taken a while for the full effect of that message to really sink in, and he had read the e-mail several more times, hoping he had missed something or had read it incorrectly. No such luck though. The words never changed. She had been ordered to deploy for real. His wife was going to war.

For the next two days, Evan reread the e-mail at least a dozen times, trying to fully understand all its realities and implications. The more he read, the more he was aware of and surprised by the cool detachment in the message's tone. She had shown no sign of excitement or fear with her words, and Evan couldn't figure that out. She had been gone for months and had just casually told him she was about to leave him for another year. It was obvious to Evan that it was getting easier all the time for Rachel to be gone and on her own, and that troubled him. He had always worked hard to try and support the things she had wanted to do and experience in the army, and he couldn't help wondering if all his encouragement had begun to come back to bite him.

Evan spent the next three weeks between her deployment news and her arrival home thinking about so many things that he felt at times like his head was swimming upstream. Everything had changed. What should he say to her? How should he feel? He had never dreamed he would be the spouse of a soldier sent to war, and he was suddenly unsure of everything. The thought of Rachel gone for five months in Guatemala had left him empty enough. Now he was being forced to face at least another year without her. How could they ever really begin to build their life together if they were never together?

CHAPTER 8

E van decided to place his first bet on the dogs. He had looked at the names and the odds but knew nothing about any of them other than what he could read quickly in the program. He remembered the first time he had ever gone to the dog races with his parents. His dad's betting lesson was that whenever in doubt, just bet on 1-5-8 together. His dad believed that system covered the inside, the outside, and the middle of the track all at once. That logic had no foundation, but for now, Evan figured it was as good as anything he could come up with so that was what he did. He decided on a trifecta again with those numbers, placed his bet, and then settled in to watch.

Evan thought dog races were incredibly fun to watch. Seeing those animals exerting every ounce of energy they had, stretching their strides to the maximum, and working so hard to catch a mechanical rabbit that would never be caught brought him pleasure. Anything or anyone who gave 100 percent impressed Evan. Maybe that was one of the reasons Evan had been so attracted to Rachel. She attacked everything full blast with all her energy and focus. When she began a project, she didn't stop until it was completed, even if that meant little or no sleep in the process. Since she possessed that level of drive as well as an eye for detail, Evan understood why she had become an outstanding soldier. Being a perfectionist also had its downside though, and during a project, Rachel could become obsessed with it and could, at times, block out everything and everyone else, including Evan. She would occasionally isolate herself for hours or even days, and if Evan could get her attention at all, it would only be for very short periods of time, and then she would return to her project.

The military readily received people who would work tirelessly to complete a task and complete it well, and Rachel fit in with them like a hand in a glove. Evan understood why she enjoyed herself so much when she put her uniform and her boots on. She received a great amount of praise and recognition from her superiors, and it is simple logic to understand that people flourish when they are appreciated just as they wither when ignored or ridiculed. Rachel's level of responsibility had risen quickly in the Guard and, with that, so did her level of enthusiasm. She could not get enough of army things, and even before she got home from Guatemala, Evan had begun to realize that he was no longer married to a teacher. He was married to a soldier.

The rabbit circled the track, and the dogs were released. Their speed was amazing, and the cheers from the spectators rose as they reached the final turn. During the stretch run, number 5 edged in front of the pack and maintained that position through the finish line. It was extremely close for second and third places, and Evan had to wait a couple extra minutes for the official results to be posted.

A short time later, the results were up on the big board. Number 8 had finished second and number 1 had come in third. Evan had won another bet. He saluted his dad's betting strategy and wore a huge smile when he saw that he had won another $226. He strolled cheerfully to the betting window to collect his winnings and tried to decide if he should press his luck or take his winnings and leave. Evan decided to head for the exit, and with more than $500 of extra money in his pocket, he was very glad he had decided to stop at the track.

Once in his car again, Evan decided to just start driving and see where he ended up. He turned left out of the racetrack and was quickly back at the main intersection he had seen two hours earlier. He then turned south just to see where that took him. He passed endless strip malls and stores, golf courses and hotels, and countless palm trees. After five miles, he saw a billboard advertising the Everglades and was immediately interested. He had seen the area on television, but now that he was this close, he wanted to see it all up close. The rest of his afternoon would be spent in a very beautiful and mysterious part of Florida. What lay ahead intrigued him, and he drove on into territory unlike any he had ever witnessed. For a moment, he allowed himself the belief that he could understand Rachel's enthusiasm regarding new sights and new places like Panama and Guatemala because he didn't know what he would soon see, but he drove on eagerly.

Even though he had no real expectations of what the Everglades looked like, he was still surprised at what unfolded before him. The highway cut through the heart of the endless marshes, and various grasses grew twenty feet high and provided refuge for countless unknown wildlife. Huge tropical trees stood proudly like sentinels guarding the egrets and osprey that made their homes high above the alligators. There was a place where one could pull his car onto the side of the highway, and Evan did that. He wanted a closer look at this amazing scenery, but after he got out of his car, an odd thought suddenly crossed his mind. There were a lot of alligators in the marsh, and they could easily be hidden very close to the road. The image of him jumping into his rented convertible with a hungry alligator in hot pursuit made him laugh, but he walked quite carefully and kept his eyes moving at all times. There were a thousand images worthy of pictures and postcards stretched out before him in every direction, and Evan's eyes scanned every direction as he tried to take it all in. Evan dared getting very near to the roadside railing because he wanted an even closer look at this vast incredible place. Again, he understood how interesting new, mysterious, and exotic things could be.

Another tourist family pulled in behind Evan's car, and they too got out for a closer look at everything. He wondered if they had considered the potential dangers like he had. Evan guessed that they were tourists because they wore the same red sunburn on their shoulders, arms, and legs that he wore. A little boy of around seven or eight years old bounced excitedly on the roadside, visibly anxious to see all the wildlife the Everglades displayed. His dad kept a close watch on the boy so that he didn't stray over the railing, but Evan could see the joy in the dad's ability to bring this experience to his son and to share it with him. Evan suddenly came to understand something he had never fully realized before. It wasn't only about experiencing the new and exciting things in life; it was having someone special to share them with. It would have been impossible to accurately describe the Everglades to a friend back home, and for the first time, he understood part of Rachel's difficulty in explaining her temporary worlds in Panama and Guatemala to him. Standing by himself on the side of the road, he knew that none of the best times in his life had ever happened while he was by himself.

CHAPTER 9

Since Rachel had driven herself to the fort back in January, Evan did not need to meet her and bring her home. She had called him from Texas and had told him the day she would be home, but he had no real idea what time that day she would pull into the driveway, and while he waited, each hour seemed like an uneasy day. Evan again had the yard manicured perfectly for her arrival, and the house was as clean and orderly as he could make it. He remembered that if she had noticed either of those things when she got home, she had failed to mention them.

She entered their house for the first time in five months, hugged Evan, and sat down on the couch. It was like she was a guest who was unsure of how to act in new surroundings. It was all oddly uncomfortable for Evan to sit there with his wife, and the conversation began as any reunion talk would. Evan started with, "I missed you. Welcome home!"

"Thanks, it's good to be back," she replied.

"I can't wait to hear about all your adventures," he continued.

"Well, I've got lots of stories, but I'm pretty tired from the flight and the drive. I started my day at five this morning," she declared with a yawn.

"Sure," stated Evan. "Get some rest, and you can tell me all about everything later on." He knew he would hear her stories soon, so he didn't press her.

Rachel continued. "I need to call Mom and let her know I'm back. She made me promise to do that."

"Okay." He walked to their home office to work on his computer, and he could overhear bits and pieces of her conversation with her mom. He sighed heavily and tried hard not to listen, but what he heard was a noticeable change in Rachel's enthusiasm and desire to talk. Forty minutes later, he had to assume that she had forgotten about her desire to take a nap, for the conversation was still going strong.

Rachel's first night at home was at best uneasy. At times, it was as if two nervous teenagers were sharing a first date. Each had obviously grown accustomed to his own nighttime routine alone and having an entire bed to himself. For Evan, several months of having just one side of the bed prior to her leaving had been replaced by sleeping in the middle of the bed and not worrying about disturbing anyone else, and there was also an unspoken pressure regarding the expectations of romance.

Evan longed for the touches, the caresses, and the kisses; but at the same time, he didn't feel comfortable initiating those things. He felt like he might somehow be invading her space, so he waited for some kind of sign from her. He never got one. He had heard enough stories of soldiers returning home from long absences and the days of passion that followed for the reunited couples, but he couldn't help but question the reality of all those stories because it didn't happen that way for Rachel and him. Nothing about their first night even resembled the mythical, romantic movie reunions. Theirs had been awkward, uncomfortable, and unsettling.

As that first night wore on and they eventually went to bed, Rachel let him see a couple yawns, once again demonstrating how tired she was, or at least how tired she wanted to appear. Evan wondered how many times he would see that same yawn in the days ahead. He already recognized it from earlier in the afternoon, right before she had talked to her mom on the telephone. He got the unspoken message, gave her a kiss, and then rolled over for what he knew would be a mostly sleepless night full of doubts, fears, and countless negative thoughts. To further fuel his already racing mind, he knew the topic of her Iraq deployment hadn't even been mentioned yet. He didn't look forward to that at all but knew it would soon be discussed at great length.

Evan had guessed correctly. His eyes would close, but his mind never disengaged. It was truly a sleepless night, and it seemed that every possible bad scenario of the army and romance together had run through his mind. He was fast becoming convinced that the two did not mix well. He even got up twice during the night, once to just watch Rachel sleep peacefully and the other time to go outside and sit on the front step. On the step, he shared the late evening solitude with the few night birds, who had chosen that time of day to sing. The summer air was warm and sticky but was still more comfortable to Evan than lying in his bed. So many things, both good and bad, crossed his mind while he sat on the edges of the silhouettes cast by a nearby streetlight. He thought of all the smiles and fun Rachel and he had shared while dating. He thought of the Labor Day phone call that had taken her to New Orleans for a month. He also thought of Panama and Guatemala, of weekend Guard drills, of changing dreams, and, eventually, he thought of Iraq and war.

He wasn't totally sure why he had felt as uncomfortable that first night Rachel got back from Guatemala, but he obviously had. He had gotten angry a few times while she had been gone because he felt like he was in the middle of a competition he couldn't win. Rachel had joined the Guard to see the world, and that was what she was doing, and he could already sense that a seemingly ordinary life at home could no longer stack up in her mind against endless new adventures in exotic and faraway places. He was physically as close to his wife as he had been for five months, yet Evan felt very alone and distant from her.

Eventually he walked quietly back into their house. His eyes had grown heavy, and he was determined to get what little sleep he could. Once in the bedroom, he inched slowly back under the covers, careful not to disturb Rachel, who was still sleeping quite peacefully. His thoughts raced too fast for peaceful sleep to be a possibility for him, but at that point, even a small bit of uneasy sleep was welcome. He glanced once at the clock and sighed heavily when he read 4:16 AM.

Morning came way too quickly for Evan, and for several minutes, he fought the urge to totally wake up. He had never been good at just lying in bed once he woke up, so he knew the battle was futile, and he rose to his feet. Rachel was still mentally on military time, so she was already up and dressed. He sauntered to the kitchen and was glad she had made coffee. He knew he looked haggard, but he also knew the coffee would help.

The conversation was warm as the two began her first full day back home. The weather was again perfect, so the two shared their coffee on the patio. The morning sunshine was powerful, and Evan was surprised at how alert he felt. After some small talk about familiar sights and home comforts, Rachel smiled and made an observation. She sipped her coffee slowly and said, "It's really nice to be wearing civilian shorts and a tank top after five straight months in my uniform and BDUs."

Evan responded, "I'll bet is. How would you like to spend your first day back home?" He had assumed that they would do something fun together to celebrate her return, and he had looked forward to whatever that might be. Even though it was still unsaid, he knew that she would only be home for a very short time, and he wanted to make all their minutes together count.

She finished her cup of coffee and rose to go inside for a refill. On her way back inside the house, she gave him her answer. "Mom is pretty anxious to see me and hear all about my trip, and she wants to spend the day with me and give her girl a hug."

When Evan heard her answer, all he could do was sigh. "So you're going to be there all day?" he hollered through the open patio door.

"More than likely," she responded. "She sounded like she had all kinds of things she wanted to do with me."

"So did I," he said coldly.

"Sorry. I already promised her I'd come pick her up, and then we'll do whatever she has lined up. I have no idea how long it will be."

Evan didn't know how to respond after that, so he just sat silently for a few more minutes then went inside. After a second cup of coffee Evan shaved, showered, and put on some shorts. While he was dressing Rachel came into the bedroom, keys in hand. "I'm heading out to see mom."

Evan was a bit surprised she was leaving that quickly. "Already? Why so early? I thought we were going to spend at least some of your first day back doing things together."

Rachel simply stated, "Mom wanted to make a day of it, so I thought I'd get an early start. We can do something tonight." She was out the door before his socks were on. He walked to the kitchen and poured his third cup of coffee and then sat in front of the television contemplating how he would now spend his day alone.

For two weeks, he had assumed he would share that day with his wife, catching up and making up for lost time, and he had no plan B. It was a beautiful morning, and after a few minutes of *The Today Show*, he decided on a round of golf. Evan truly enjoyed golf, and one of his greatest pleasures had been teaching the game to Rachel. She had learned quickly, and it had become something he thought they could enjoy and share even as an old married couple.

Evan returned home five hours later with fifteen extra dollars he had won during the round. His enthusiasm faded a bit when he rounded the corner near his house and saw an empty driveway. She wasn't home yet. He decided he still had time to do something special to mark Rachel's return to him, so he drove to the grocery store to buy some thick pork chops and other things he planned to prepare for a romantic meal for two. Just planning the meal excited Evan. He liked to cook, but it was never as fun cooking meals for himself as it was cooking for two. For months, the kitchen had been a bland, necessary room; but that afternoon, it came to life with slicing, chopping, and the aromas of Evan's favorite seasonings. He had it all planned out in his mind. He would call her after a while and find out what time she would be home, and then he would have everything prepared and set out on the table just as she walked through the door. He could already picture her smile.

Evan called her around 5:00 and casually asked what time she thought she would be home. She told him she would get there around 7:30, so he planned accordingly. He cut the potatoes, steamed the broccoli, made the salads, and started cooking the pork chops so they would be properly cooked at just the right time. He wanted everything to be perfect. He set the table, monitored the food, and he hoped his timing would be as excellent as he wanted it to be. He was certain she would appreciate his effort, and he looked forward to sharing their first meal together in a very long time.

Evan began clock-watching … 7:25 … 7:28 … 7:36 … 7:45 … All the enthusiasm he had initially possessed began to fade with each passing minute. The entire meal had been ready to serve for twenty minutes, but Rachel was not there … 7:55 … 8:10 … Excitement could no longer be found anywhere in Evan. It had been replaced with an amazing amount of frustration and disappointment. He wanted to call her and find out what had happened, but he decided against that. She would get there when she got there. He had already called her once.

At 8:30, Evan totally gave up. He was angry at Rachel's lack of consideration, and he was angry that his plan and his effort had gone to waste. It had all been ruined, and at that point, only he knew that. He decided that even though he couldn't pull off the special evening he had wanted to, he could make sure she knew that he had tried. He put all the food on the plates and then cleaned up the biggest part of the kitchen mess. The table looked like it had been set up for a romantic meal at a classy restaurant, and that was exactly what he wanted.

At 9:00, Rachel pulled into the driveway, a full hour and a half later than she had promised. Evan sat on the couch and didn't say anything when she walked into the living room. He just sat with his eyes on the television. She smiled and said, "That was fun. Mom and I had a great day." His eyes met hers, but he did not reply. He knew he would have his say very soon.

She walked straight to the bathroom, and Evan hollered to her. "Are you hungry?"

She responded through the wall. "Mom and I went out to eat. That's why I was l was later than I said I'd be."

Evan's anger boiled, but he held it in for the moment. He waited. It took another few minutes before she walked toward the kitchen to get a drink, and she stopped in her tracks when she saw the dining room table fully set and the plates sitting there filled with cold food. Evan could tell she wasn't quite sure what to say at that moment, but he waited silently. There was no way he was going to speak first.

She returned with a can of pop and a puzzled look on her face. She told him the table looked great, and she asked him, "Why didn't you eat?"

Evan was amazed at the question. "Are you serious? Why didn't I eat alone? Don't you get it at all? Can you not see that I tried to do something special for you, and your first thought was that I should have just eaten by myself? The whole reason I did all that was for you. I wanted to make your first night back home memorable with a nice meal together. You have a cell phone. If you were going to be an hour and a half later than you said, I wish you would have called me."

She looked at Evan and then back at the table full of food. "You could have called me too and told me you were cooking a meal."

"I did call and took you at your word that you'd be here at 7:30. Remember?"

"I guess I spoiled your plans then. What do you want me to say?"

"Nothing." Evan got off the couch and walked to the dining room. He began clearing the table and threw away the entire meal loudly, making sure she heard everything falling into the trash. When the food and the kitchen were cleaned up, he walked back into the living room wearing a wry smile. He coldly told her, "I'll be back in a few minutes." And he made his way to his car. Ten minutes later, he returned carrying a McDonald's sack and a cup of iced tea. He passed through the living room without a word and marched directly into the dining room. He opened the sack and set his hamburger on the table. Rachel remained in the living room, and he hoped she could feel the full effect of his frustration through the wall. He had become all too familiar with sitting alone at that table eating a hamburger by himself, but this one tasted a lot worse than usual to him. To say that Evan enjoyed any part of Rachel's first full day at home would be a lie. His emotions had traveled a great distance, covering the entire spectrum from doubt to anticipation and excitement and then to anger and frustration, finally ending back where he had begun, doubting everything he was living through. The second night together was no better than the first, and Evan could only wonder what lay ahead for the rest of Rachel's short stopover at home before she headed to war.

CHAPTER 10

The afternoon Florida sunshine again reminded Evan of the newness of his sunburn. He could feel it on his arms and on the backs of his legs. The family was still enjoying the Everglades wildlife along the roadside when Evan climbed back into his convertible and continued his drive to the south. The scenery was still impressive, but it didn't vary much. The vastness of the marshy wasteland stretched on mile after mile, seemingly without end, and as unique and beautiful as it was, Evan found it hard to imagine living there. Evan drove for another fifteen miles before he came to a trading post. He was sure it was a tourist trap, but he enjoyed souvenirs and mementos of new places he visited, so he stopped and went inside. He looked like all the other customers and simply blended in quite inconspicuously as he began shopping. Of course, there were the T-shirts, hundreds of them. He thumbed through several stacks, trying to find one without an alligator picture on it, and before long, he moved to the hats and other souvenirs that included rows of shells, ashtrays, shot glasses, and more.

The shot glasses held Evan's attention the longest of anything he saw. He did not collect them, but Rachel did, or at least she used to. They had been reminders of the many trips Rachel and he had shared, and in six short years, the collection had grown rather large. She never settled for any shot glasses either. She actually shopped for the best one, the one she felt best represented their trip. Her shelf at home had displayed shot glasses from at least four Nevada towns, including Las Vegas, Reno, Elko, and Winnemucca. There were also reminders of visits to Atlanta, Green Bay, Minneapolis, New Orleans, and, of course, several honeymoon glasses from Myrtle Beach. Evan could still remember each of those trips vividly. To him the best thing about every one of them was the fact they had been together and had shared them. He looked around the store and was again reminded that now he was by himself.

He almost bought an Everglades shot glass but chose not to. He did not collect them, Rachel did. He walked past the ashtrays and shirts and headed back out into the sunshine without buying anything. He had no idea where he would eventually end up, but he felt he was doing himself some good to think about all these things and try and sort out some of his frustration and confusion. He had come to Florida this weekend to think things through and try and start his life again, and he felt like he was making some progress in that direction. He thought he might be the only tourist in the area without any souvenirs, but that was all right with him. This was not a souvenir trip. He steered his convertible back onto Highway 41 and drove back north into Naples. The heat still felt great on his body, and he had already grown to really like the feel of the breeze on his body as he drove down the road with the car top down. When he passed the spot where he had previously stopped along the roadside, he saw two new sets of families enjoying the view. He honked his horn at them for no real reason and drove on past them.

Before long, he found himself back in the heart of Naples. For a moment, he thought about returning to the dog track, but instead, he answered the signals being sent to him by his stomach. He could see a sign up ahead for Applebee's, and it didn't take long to decide to stop and eat there. Applebee's had been and probably still was Rachel's favorite place to eat, and as Evan pulled into the parking lot, he realized he had not eaten at one for at least two years.

It was midafternoon, so the restaurant wasn't full like it surely would be a few hours later. There was plenty of room at the bar, but Evan chose to sit at a table. The menu was basically the same as the

Applebee's back home, and though he usually chose a salad or a pasta dish, this time he ordered a large steak. His entire ordering process took about ten seconds as it usually did with him. He could never understand why people turned ordering a meal into a personal scavenger hunt. "Can I substitute this for that?" "Can I get half of this and extra of that?" "Can I have this but on the side?" "Can I have it without the bun?" He couldn't imagine that every once in a while, what was offered on the menu couldn't actually be good enough just as it was. He had come to the conclusion that some people simply enjoyed complicating things, perhaps out of habit, whether it was ordering a meal, dealing with others, or living their lives.

The background music was a variety of oldies, which pleased Evan. He was a huge fan of '70s music, and since it was not crowded, the music could be easily heard. At the moment, it was Peter, Paul, and Mary's turn and they smoothly sang:

> *Kiss me and smile for me, tell me that you'll wait for me*
> *Hold me like you'll never let me go, I'm leaving on a jet plane,*
> *Don't know when I'll be back again …*

The steak was delicious, a perfect medium-well with incredible flavor. Evan ate slowly and savored every bite until his plate was empty. The waitress filled his tea glass twice and then brought him the bill. Several others had come in while Evan was eating, and the restaurant was now nearly half full. Families and couples waited with great enthusiasm to enjoy their meals and to get a short break from the blazing afternoon sunshine. Evan watched a couple in their forties, who were smiling, talking, and holding hands, and he knew it was time for him to leave. He paid for his meal and quietly left.

The sun was so bright it made Evan squint when he first walked outside. He stood next to his car for a minute, deciding where to go and what to do next. That moment was another instant reminder that he was there alone and invisible, and he knew that no one in Naples or

Fort Myers cared what he did. He drove west out of Naples and crossed the bridge back into Fort Myers Beach. Traffic was reasonably heavy so it took him a little longer to get there, but it didn't matter. He had come to know that when a person had no plans and no real purpose, time became relatively meaningless.

Time had become such a puzzling concept for Evan. Not long ago, he had looked forward to years of smiles and fun and sharing with Rachel, but outside forces had changed all that. It was an odd paradox to him that time had become both precious and pointless almost at the same time. Every day that Rachel had been gone seemed like a waste to him, time that could never be retrieved, yet when she was back home and they were together, even though those minutes and days were few and important, they were not valued or nurtured or spent well.

He viewed the two weeks Rachel was home from Guatemala as mostly wasted. Minutes and hours that should have been gold bars had been tossed away like pennies. He was angry at her for not missing him more and not wanting every minute possible with him while she was home, and he was angry at himself for not making his thoughts more known to her. Had her e-mails from Guatemala been lies when she wrote "Miss you"? He wondered about that every day. His days at home both with her there and with her gone had felt a lot like this weekend in Florida. He felt invisible, unimportant, and totally without purpose.

The convertible finally reached Fort Myers Beach, and he found a parking spot, grabbed his towel, and headed to the sand to continue his sunburn. On such a sunny Saturday afternoon, the beach was extremely crowded. He laid his towel down on the first empty space he came to, took off his sandals, and lay on his back. He slid off his shirt and decided to be courageous enough to get some sun on his stomach too.

To his left, he saw a group of twenty-something men daring each other to brave the water and generally having a good, loud time. He thought that the vast majority of soldiers Rachel spent her time with were as young as this group or even younger. He watched their behavior, which was harmless enough but a bit immature for a crowded beach.

It was plain to see that it would only take the slightest suggestion to turn their words and actions into far cruder things than he watched and heard at the moment. He could vaguely remember how he spoke and acted at their age, and he knew being around young guys in a military environment had to have rubbed off on Rachel, both for good and bad.

On his right, there were two young ladies obviously enjoying the chance to work on their tans, and their skimpy bikinis showed as much of their bodies as Florida law would allow. Evan looked around and saw that he wasn't the only guy on the beach who had noticed this pair, and their smiles and giggles suggested that they wanted and liked the attention they drew. Right next to the girls were two small children building a sandcastle complete with a moat. Evan smiled at their innocence and tried his best to remember what that felt like. One of the children had a shovel full of wet sand and was flipping it into the air much like a chef flipping a burger on his spatula.

The two bikini-clad college girls turned over in an attempt to keep their tans even. Every movement the pair made got the attention of a large number of the male beachgoers, including Evan. Every few minutes, he could hear a giggle from the pair, and he felt certain they knew they were being admired and that they enjoyed the ego boost they were receiving. Evan, for the most part, just sat and quietly watched people. The beach was crowded with every size, shape, and type of person imaginable, each enjoying his own method of soaking up the beautiful Florida winter day. A few of the bravest ones ventured into the water but rarely went further than waist deep. Frisbees and footballs filled the air, and Evan sat on his towel and watched it all. The tops of his legs were pink from the sun, but he didn't mind. A bit of discomfort right then was a small price to pay to be able to show off a winter tan back home. He wondered how many of the people he saw sleeping on their towels would also pay for their sunburn the next day.

CHAPTER 11

On Rachel's fifth day at home from Guatemala, the topic of Iraq was finally discussed. Evan had still not heard many details of her time in Guatemala, and with Rachel's mind now focused on Iraq, he understood he probably would never hear much more about her past few months. He had learned to curb his curiosity because she was very much a one-thing-at-a-time person, and now it was time for Iraq. He couldn't figure out if she didn't want him to know about her trip or whether it was truly already out of her thoughts as she looked ahead to going to war. Evan could only imagine the apprehension that would bring to anyone's thoughts.

She had been very busy on her computer for nearly two straight days, and almost everything she did there was army related. Her iTunes kept her company as she typed and made phone call after phone call doing what she had to do in order to prepare to be gone for a year. Evidently, she finally had everything in order and was ready to include Evan and let him know what was going on. The two sat at the dining room table, Evan with a glass of tea and Rachel with a stack of papers she had printed out. The military definitely had its own way of doing things, much of which Evan did not understand. He knew he was about to find out a lot more, however, which wouldn't take much because up to that point, he had been mostly in the dark on any details.

It didn't take long for Evan to be overwhelmed with information.

In a matter of minutes, he had gone from knowing next to nothing to hearing more than he could absorb in one sitting. Rachel began her explanations. "I've set up all my personal bills on automatic payments so you won't have to do anything with them. All my insurances, car payments, and credit card stuff has been set up that way."

Evan hadn't even considered all those things. "That's good because I wouldn't have known where all those things were."

"I know, but it's taken care of so you won't have to worry about them. I also have a will I made and some power-of-attorney forms you need to sign. You should probably get around to making your will too. I know we've talked about it, but I had to do one since I'm going on active duty."

"I know I should," answered Evan. "I guess I can do that sometime soon."

"The power of attorney is the biggie. If something happens to me over there then you can take care of everything that would be in my name. There are also some other benefits you get while I'm on active duty. You get more life insurance and perks at the fort and so on. We can go through those later."

"That's fine. It's gonna take a while to absorb all this anyway."

"Yeah, it's a lot, but I'm required to have all this stuff in order before I go. That's what I've been doing the past couple days, and I think I have it all. I'm supposed to make it so that you don't have anything extra of mine to worry about while I'm gone."

"You mean anything other than you getting killed, right?" He found it a bit ironic that the army arranged things so that the only thing a spouse at home had left to worry about was his loved one being killed in a war zone. He did his best to comprehend all she tried to explain to him, but he knew he would have to look over all the material again.

Rachel laughed. "Yeah, I guess I don't have a form to take care of that worry, but I'll be fine."

After thirty minutes of forms and explanations, Rachel finally began to talk about her duty. She didn't fully know exactly what she would be assigned to do, but she had a general idea. "I'll be in Baghdad in a section of Camp Victory, a huge base set up as a central point for troops. I'll be working in communications in some way, but I don't know for sure what my job will be."

Evan looked curiously. "Communications can mean a thousand different things. You don't know any more than that?"

"Not yet. That's all I know right now, but I think I'll be in an office somewhere on post, which is a good thing."

Evan continued his questions. "Do you know where you'll be living? I'm picturing a huge circus tent like you had in New Orleans for the hurricane cleanup."

They both laughed at that memory. "No, I'll be in a trailer that holds two people, so I'll have a roommate. Some of my fellow soldiers, who have been there already, told me about the trailers. They said there was enough space for two twin beds and a little bit of space to hang uniforms but not much more. They aren't fancy, but they are air-conditioned, so I'll be able to get some breaks from the heat while I sleep, and I'll also have some privacy, much more than I had in New Orleans for sure!"

Evan interrupted, "Any idea what your day-to-day routine will be or what Camp Victory is like?"

She grinned with an odd sort of pride and answered. "A little. I'll have a bulletproof vest and an M-16 that I'll have to have with me every time I step outside a building." He found no comfort in that statement at all. He could barely imagine a daily situation like that and was amazed at how she appeared eager to embrace it.

The last piece of information Rachel shared hit Evan like a truck. "Oh, and there is one more kind of big thing," she continued. "While I was in Guatemala, my unit was already sent to Wisconsin to begin their training for Iraq. I want to make sure I am fully prepared when I get over there and can't stand the idea of being behind in the training, so part of my last two days was spent moving up my departure date."

Evan could only imagine how blank the expression on his face was.

"Really? After six months gone and being home for less than two weeks, you requested leaving early? So when do you go?"

"In three days."

"Three days? Damn! And then you'll be gone for a year. I don't know what to say. I understand you not wanting to be behind your unit with the training, but it's still disappointing. I guess the worst part is how anxious you are to leave here again." Then Evan sat silently, not knowing what to think or feel.

"I have no control about being deployed," Rachel continued. "But now that I know I'm going, I want to do my job really well."

"It's obvious you're excited about all this," said Evan. "I wish I could share that enthusiasm, but I can't. It scares me."

"I'll be fine," she stated as reassuringly as possible. "I don't know what I'll get into there, but it's my turn to go. I always knew this was possible when I joined the Guard, and I'm ready to do my part."

He was also disappointed at how apparently apathetic she was to his doubts, worries, and fears. She knew he was a deep thinker, and he couldn't figure out why she didn't realize that he had concerns too. It now seemed that her only thoughts were of things immediately related to her alone. Maybe she was just trying to act tough to help ease his worries, but if that were the case, she did not succeed.

"So what would you like to do for your last three days at home?" he asked. It was the only thing he could think of to say.

"I don't know. I've been so busy with everything I haven't really given it any thought." He managed a small smile and walked out into the backyard. He didn't believe her. He knew her too well, and she planned everything in her mind. The discussion at the table was finished.

Some of the initial level of being uncomfortable together in the house had subsided but had not disappeared. They had shared just a couple meals, with Evan doing the cooking, but it was not the same as before she had left. It seemed that Rachel's eating habits had dramatically changed while she was in Guatemala. She certainly ate a lot less and was far more interested in salads and granola bars than in burgers and steaks. Most nights, Rachel didn't eat at all, so Evan found himself once again cooking just for himself. Even though his wife was home, things didn't feel much different to him than when she was gone.

The day after the talk at the table, Rachel told Evan that she would like to go out to eat and have a farewell meal with her mom, her two brothers, and their families. Evan thought that sounded like a good idea, so he made sure he was ready to leave when the time arrived. She and her mom had already lined it all up, and the time and place had been set for the gathering. It would be the night before she left for Wisconsin to begin her training for deployment.

The group all arrived within ten minutes of each other, and they got the waitress to set up a large table for fourteen people. Rachel sat between her mom and her younger brother, and Evan sat opposite her. The talk was light and lively and all rightly centered around Rachel and her departure. Her mom tried her best to be cheerful but did not succeed. Her worry was at times worn openly on her face no matter how hard she attempted to disguise it. Rachel's brothers and their children were more laid back about everything. They were as used to not seeing Rachel as Evan had become, so they joined in at times but seemed more interested in the meal ahead of them.

As with many family gatherings, it seemed that often everyone was talking at once. Evan waited patiently for his food, catching bits and pieces of the conversation going on around him.

"Man, it's been hot lately, hasn't it?"

"For sure. I hate being out in it every day."

"Look at that guy over there. Can you imagine having hair that looks like that?"

"Don't you just love the strawberry shakes here? I've been waiting all day for one of those."

He could hear parts of what Rachel and her mom were saying across the table, and it seemed they were talking about food and cooking. It all seemed very casual, and then he heard a sentence from Rachel that instantly made his eyes turn cold. She leaned in close to her mom and said, "I haven't eaten many meals at home because the skillet he cooks with is so worn out I can taste the Teflon in the food." The two shared a long private laugh at Evan's expense, and he knew they believed he had not heard the comment. Any desire Evan might have had to be cheerful had left him, and he wanted to simply get up and leave right then.

Behind his calm face, he was silently fuming and humiliated. He couldn't imagine his wife showing joy at making him look bad, and she had done it with such ease. If she was that bold with him at the same table, how often did she find other ways to slam him when he wasn't around? He had always tried to build her up to others, and his disappointment in her words was so great it could not be measured. Maybe the comment was a joke, but he felt a great amount of hurt from it.

At the end of the meal, hugs were exchanged. Rachel's family knew she was leaving again for a long time, and they did their best to make sure she knew she would be missed.

"Keep your head down, sis," said one of her brothers.

The kids joined in as well. "We'll miss you, Aunt Rachel."

The last farewell was with her mom. "I'll pray for you every day, and I know you'll be safe. I have to believe that."

Rachel tried to reassure her. "I will be safe. Don't worry. I can take care of myself, and I've been trained well for what I'll be doing. Besides, I'm not heading to Baghdad yet. I'll just be in Wisconsin."

After the final hug, everyone piled into his car and headed home. Evan was very quiet as he drove, and he turned up the radio in hopes of discouraging conversation during their drive back to the house. Rachel closed her eyes and either rested or acted like she was resting. Either was fine with Evan. It was late, and he was tired too, but more than that, he was still hurt and angry and embarrassed.

When they got home and got into the house, Rachel again showed him a big yawn. "I'm heading to bed. I'm beat," she stated without any emotion at all. "That was a lot of fun." Evan did not reply. Instead, he went to the kitchen and grabbed a beer. He then opened the cupboard, found the skillet Rachel and her mom had laughed about, and threw it away. It would never cook another meal. After the skillet was disposed of, he took his beer in hand and went out to sit on the front step. As with previous nights, he sat with the night birds and the streetlights in an attempt to lessen his anger.

Three beers and at least an hour later, Evan decided to go to bed. He was intentionally silent as he undressed and slid under the sheet. For a short while, he lay on his side, watching Rachel sleep, looking at her with new eyes and wondering if he even knew her anymore. He had grown accustomed to sleepless nights the past ten days, but that night, the beer had helped slow his thinking down, and before long, he was snoring.

Rachel's last day at home was a blur of activity, with final packing and a host of small loose ends she wanted to tie up. The military seemed to like to do things very early in the morning, and her flight to Wisconsin was set to leave at 6:30 AM the following morning. She again wanted to leave in the late afternoon so she could wake up and already be on base. Since this was not her final deployment, she would drive herself to the fort. She would train there for five to six weeks, come home for four days, and then her entire group would leave for Iraq.

Evan helped her load a year's worth of uniforms, socks, and other essentials, which would be shipped overseas separately, and when everything was in her vehicle, there was barely enough room for her to sit. They stood together yet again in the driveway as she prepared to leave him. Evan could feel the déjà vu and spoke up. "It seems like we spend a lot of time here getting ready for you to leave me."

Rachel apparently thought he was making a joke. "It is kind of getting like a routine, isn't it? Oh well, you're probably so used to being by yourself now that you like that better than when I'm here."

Evan gave her a strange look. "I don't think so. I didn't marry you so that I could be by myself all the time. I know you've told me over and over that you'll always come back to me whenever you put on the uniform and leave, but I guess I thought your time here would be more permanent and not just a lot of temporary stopovers."

"It will be that way eventually, but I've got to go now. I'll be back for a few days after the training is done."

"I'll be here waiting," he spoke without any great emotion.

"Deal," she replied. Then she kissed him good-bye, and he stood in the driveway to watch her drive out of sight yet again. He had grown to hate the driveway routine, and he slowly walked to the door and went inside to begin the next quiet stretch of time as a single married man.

The quiet in the living room surrounded him, and he felt it closing in. Evan knew he could deal with the silence and the solitude. He had been forced to do it before. The part that made him sad was he now realized the tension in the house that had been everywhere while Rachel was home was totally absent. He hated that he felt that way, and he desperately wanted it to be different. None of this was what he had signed on for and dreamed of when he had first realized that he wanted to spend the rest of his life with Rachel. Like before, he tried hard to push all the doubts from his thoughts, even though he knew he would never be totally successful.

She wasn't in a war zone yet. It was only Wisconsin and training. He told himself those things over and over. Evan knew the five or six weeks ahead would fly by, and then the true realities of having a wife in Iraq would stare him in the face. For now, all he knew was that he was alone again, and he didn't like it one bit. The military did a great job of lining up paperwork and logistical details, but Evan wished someone could figure out a way to help him deal with the emotional aspects of being apart from his wife. He was in his forties and was struggling with things he believed he was mature enough to handle. He could truly empathize with a couple in their twenties in a similar situation. For the first time, military separation had become a stark reality for Evan instead of a vague abstraction that only affected others. A short year earlier, he believed his life had been on the road he had longed to travel, and he had been incredibly excited about the endless possibilities of the journey. Now he was alone and frustrated and helpless to change the roadblocks in his path. He could see some of the impediments that lay ahead of him, but he was unsure just how high they would eventually get. He was even more afraid of what waited for him on the other side of the roadblocks he could see because he felt certain there were larger hurdles waiting to greet him even further down the road. Sitting on his couch, he now understood their potential to be really large and difficult to conquer. Everything in his world was changing so quickly, and he saw no way to corral those changes or even slow them down.

CHAPTER 12

After a decent night's sleep, Evan rose to another stunning summer morning. His first thought was that Rachel was on her way to her Wisconsin destination and would soon begin settling in to start her training for war. He could not even visualize the environment and the routine she would have there, and he knew he would, at best, learn only a portion of it anyway from talking to her. He finally settled for realizing that whatever she would get into there would make her happy, and he found a smile with that thought. He stepped outside, coffee in hand, and greeted his neighbor next door. The neighbor was preparing to mow his yard, which made Evan look harder at his own grass, and he decided he would mow his as well. At least that would kill two hours of his day, and he would worry about the rest of the day after that.

A couple hours later, Evan's lawn was as perfectly cut and trimmed as he could make it, and as he gave his work a final look, he beamed with pride. It always gave him at least a temporary sense of accomplishment, and at that point in his life, he looked for all those moments he could find. For the biggest part of his life, purpose had never been an issue for him. He had always known his purpose and had worked hard to achieve success. The last year, however, had been very different for him, and for the first time in his memory, he had begun to doubt everything about his goals, his dreams, and his purpose.

He had previously viewed his life like a miner's scale, with all his talents and aspirations on one side and Rachel's on the other. Until her New Orleans trip, the two sides of the scale had been level, with each side serving as a perfectly balanced support for the other side. Whenever one side dipped a little, the other side worked to regain the balance. It was all unspoken, but it worked nicely. For quite a while now, he had felt the balance shifting, and no matter how hard he tried, he could not come up with a way to once again get the two sides even.

From their first date, Evan and Rachel had been a great match, though there had been a few trying times along the way. After their first date, Evan knew he wanted to spend a lot more time with her. He had been instantly captivated by her looks, her personality, and her smile. The only immediate problem he could see was that she had also been dating another man. Once Evan learned that detail, he asked her to stop seeing the other guy and date him exclusively. She had agreed to do that, and their beginning was underway.

The other troubling time should have been more of a warning for Evan than it had been at the time. After a year and a half of serious dating, Rachel suddenly told him that she wanted to break up and be on her own. Her reasons were vague, but she left her home and moved to an apartment on base fifty miles away. She commuted each day to teach and then drove back to actively pursue the military things she wanted to explore. This arrangement lasted five months and became Evan's first real taste of finishing second to the army. During those five months, Evan had no idea what Rachel's daily life was like, and he certainly had no way of knowing what she was thinking. What he did know was how he felt. He missed her and wanted her back, if that was possible. He had heard through a mutual friend that she had been dating another soldier, whom she had met on base, but he never found out for sure if that had been true. He figured he had nothing to lose, so he took action and decided to find out one way or the other if there was a chance of getting back together with her.

He called Rachel's mom, and the two talked a while, catching up on each other's lives. "How are you?" began Evan. "I've missed talking with you and just wanted to see how everything is going."

Her mom politely responded, "I'm just fine. Everything is just going along like it should. You know how it is. Nothing ever really changes here."

"Things not changing can be a very good thing sometimes," Evan added. "There's something to be said for knowing what to expect."

'That's very true," she said. "I had a hunch I might be hearing from you before long."

"Oh really? Why did you think that?"

"I just had a feeling."

"Smart mom," he laughed. "I guess you have figured out that I'm missing your daughter, and I figured you would be the one to talk to first to find out if you think there is any chance of us getting back together."

"I miss her too. I hate her being clear up at the fort and not closer, but that's what she thought she wanted. I don't know what to tell you, and I certainly can't speak for her, but my guess is that she's missing you a bit too. My best advice is to just give her a call on her cell phone and tell her what you just told me."

"Okay, that's probably what I'll do. Thanks for the advice, and it was nice talking with you again."

"You too. Good luck," she said and then she hung up the phone.

He was sure Rachel and her mom would talk and that Rachel would learn of Evan's call, so he decided to wait a few days before calling her. Three days later, it took Evan three beers to summon up the nerve to call her. He felt like a nervous high school boy making a prom call. He really wanted her back, but he also knew the risk he was taking with the call. He realized that if she liked things as they currently were then the two of them as a couple could more than likely be permanently finished. One thing in life Evan despised was living in limbo, and at that point, he believed that even a no from her would be preferable to constantly wondering and never knowing for sure whether or not they could go forward.

When Rachel answered the phone, Evan swallowed hard and began. "Hi. Have you got some time to talk a bit?"

"Sure, what's up?" she answered casually.

"I just thought I'd call and see how things were going for you up there."

"It's different actually living on post, but it's all right," she stated. "And the drive isn't so bad each morning. It gives me some time to relax and get ready for my days at school."

"Well," Evan stammered, "the real reason I called is to tell you that I miss you, and if you'd like, I would enjoy taking you to dinner sometime soon. I'd like to talk with you and catch up but not on the phone." He waited for her answer and wondered what ran through her mind before she gave it.

She answered fairly quickly and said, "Dinner would be fine. I'll check my schedule and get back to you, okay?"

"Sounds great," answered Evan with a huge silent smile on his face.

When they hung up the phones, he smiled that the conversation he had stressed over was done. Time would tell how things would eventually work out.

Four days after Evan called her, Rachel called him back. He was both nervous and excited but was ready to hear whatever she had to tell him. To Evan's surprise, the conversation was relatively short.

Rachel began. "My family is all getting together at a nice restaurant in three days, and I'd like to invite you to join us. Saturday night, around 7:00 at Jackson's Restaurant if you want to come."

It wasn't exactly the private dinner he had imagined, and he was a bit surprised by how formal she sounded with the invitation, but he figured she would be more comfortable with others from her family nearby, so he accepted. To him it was a chance at another beginning with her, and he welcomed that under any circumstances. "I'd love to," he responded. "I'll be there."

The three days leading up to the meal were a minor eternity for Evan. Some of what he had thought of saying to her would now change because they would not be alone. On his way to meet Rachel and her family, he decided to just let the evening unfold and keep things light. This was a time to get reacquainted, truly a time to just dip his toes into the water. The previous comfort level between the two was there from the start of the night, and the meal went well. Evan and Rachel agreed to talk again soon, and everyone went his separate way after the food had been finished. Evan had a thirty-minute drive home, and he spent most of it smiling.

The weeks that Rachel was in Wisconsin were far more filled with apprehension than Evan had anticipated they would be. His nights were restless, and many of his worries and fears had spilled over into his daytime thoughts. The full weight of his wife going to war had begun to totally sink in. All he had to base his mental images on were the stories he had seen on the news, and the thoughts of her dealing daily with rockets, missiles, roadside bombs, snipers, and more overwhelmed him at times. Even though Evan was naturally an optimistic guy, the potential dangers she would soon face had him greatly concerned. He knew she was tough, but tough wasn't always enough to survive. A lot of tough soldiers throughout history had died in wars.

If Rachel was nervous or fearful, she never showed it to him. Her e-mails and phone calls from Wisconsin were always enthusiastic, and her anticipation for heading to Iraq only seemed to grow. He wondered if all she said to him was genuine because he could not imagine heading to a war zone with no fears or doubts or worries. Talking tough and acting tough were both well and good, but even Evan knew that Rachel would soon be thrown into the middle of a reality that training alone could not completely prepare anyone for.

All the war thoughts were mixed in Evan's mind with Rachel's two confusing and frustrating weeks at home. Every moment of that time should have been a treasure, but instead, it had been mostly wasted and filled with awkward hours.

She would be home again for four days before her official deployment, and he wondered often how those days would go. He hoped with all his heart they would be better than her recent two weeks with him.

One of the days Rachel was gone to Wisconsin was her birthday. Evan was at a loss as to how to celebrate that with her from a distance, just like he had been made to do on both their anniversaries. He wanted to do special, clever, creative things for her on those special days, but he couldn't because she was gone and not with him. He had to settle for a cheerful e-mail wishing her well and a phone call that night that lasted thirty minutes. He knew they were both missing out, but he didn't know what he could do to change any of that.

Images of Rachel going to war never left Evan's mind no matter what he did. If he mowed the lawn or watched television or just drove down the road, his thoughts always turned to the dangers she would soon face. He watched the news every day to learn more about the current situation in Iraq and specifically in Baghdad, and those reports did little to lessen his fears. He saw many reports of bombings and raids and roadside bombings. There were daily casualties, and it seemed to Evan that danger lurked in every corner of Baghdad. He also knew that he would never know the daily realities she would be thrown into, partly because she would not or could not tell him. No matter how he looked at what lay ahead, he didn't like what he saw.

In mid-August, Rachel e-mailed Evan that her unit's training was nearly completed and that she would be home soon for those four days before officially shipping out to Iraq. Like her last two arrivals home, Evan had the lawn looking perfect, and he had the house spotless. Part of him hoped that she would at least comment on his efforts this time. She had failed to do that on her previous returns home, but he had everything looking great anyway. The day she was to come home, Evan felt the same nerves he had experienced when she returned from Guatemala. He knew in his heart that the emotions would be different and more intense this time. It was not the same leaving for a construction job in a peaceful country as it was leaving for active-duty service in a war, and until she pulled into the driveway and the four short days were shared, all Evan could do was wonder what both of them would say, feel, and do.

CHAPTER 13

Rachel's four days at home were again a flurry of constant activity. Evan figured she was full of nervous energy and anticipation, and he decided that constant activity was her way of dealing with that. She had several loads of laundry to do, which was followed by carefully packing everything in the limited luggage space she was allowed. All she was allowed was a carry-on, so she had her backpack stuffed full. She spent parts of each day with her mom, made numerous phone calls to friends, and tied up every loose end she could think of. Her urgency was visibly evident, and Evan mostly stayed out of her way. He was not the one going to war, and he didn't even pretend to know what Rachel was thinking as her few days at home rushed by. He wished she would have shared some of her thoughts with him, but she chose not to do that.

Deployment day came, and Rachel appeared ready. This time, Evan drove her to the fort. It was extremely important to him to be an active part of her deployment ceremony, and there was no way he would not have been there with her. It was a typical Midwest August day. The sun was bearing down, and the breeze was absent, but none of the three hundred or so people at the airport hangar on base seemed to mind the heat because their thoughts were all uniformly directed toward things like war, danger, fear, loneliness, and a dozen other unspoken emotions.

All the soldiers who were deploying had to report several hours

ahead of their flight's take-off time, and after each one had gotten
checked in, he had the rest of the time to visit with family and friends.
Rachel got checked in early and had all her paperwork requirements
cleared, so she and Evan had two final hours to spend together. It would
be many months before the two could be together again, and Evan
knew all too well what that meant for him.

Rachel was unsure about the quality of the food on her upcoming
marathon trip across the ocean, and she had been told it would be
approximately a twenty-hour flight, so she and Evan drove to a nearby
Wendy's on base to grab a meal. There were others from the unit there
too, smiling anxiously as they prepared to say good-bye to their families.
Evan and Rachel talked about communication options while she was in
Iraq and about the things he could send her once she was settled in.

"I know you told me that Camp Victory has a reasonably large PX,
but I'm still thinking there might be things you want or need that they
don't have."

"Possibly," she answered, "but I won't know that until I get there."

"I guess that's true," Evan agreed. "I don't think you'll be needing a
parka anytime soon, so I won't worry about sending you one of those."

"No kidding!" she exclaimed. "It does get cold over there in the
winter, but it's gonna be really hot for a long time before that arrives."
They both knew that in a few days, she would be in the scorching desert
heat. There would be many days in her immediate future that would be
hotter than the hottest summer day in the Midwest. "I hope like hell my
trailer air conditioner works like it's supposed to." Evan could certainly
understand that desire.

Time raced by, and soon they both knew they needed to go back
to the airport hangar. Going to eat did not stop the clock from ticking
away the final minutes before Rachel and her unit flew off to war. The
trip to Wendy's had just been the last diversion before the final roll call
and lineup was called. The parking lot was full, and there was a steady
stream of people filing into the hangar. It was almost time.

Rachel went to ask a fellow soldier a question about something, which gave Evan a chance to watch how others were reacting to the moment. He was not surprised by what he saw. Tears flowed freely from the wives and mothers, who could bottle their emotions no longer. There were hugs everywhere, and fathers beamed with pride, no doubt keeping their true concerns hidden in order to look strong for their children. The entire hangar was thick with emotion, both visible and invisible. He took notice of a quiet, demure young woman near him. She was visibly emotional, and Evan stuck up a conversation with her.

"Which soldier is yours?" he inquired.

It took a second for her to realize that Evan was talking to her. "That one over there," she replied, pointing to a tall, athletic young man, who was busy with his fellow soldiers.

"Your husband?" Evan continued.

"Yeah. What about you?"

He found Rachel in the crowd and pointed her out to the woman. "That's my wife."

"Are you scared for her?" the woman continued.

Her bluntness caught him somewhat off guard, but this was not a day for holding true emotions and feelings inside. He answered her quickly. "Yes, I am. I have no idea what she will be getting into."

"I'm scared too," she said softly, trying to disguise the tears she wiped from her eyes. "He keeps telling me he'll be fine, but he can't know that. I wish he didn't have to go."

"I understand completely," reassured Evan. "I guess it's time to believe in them and trust their training and their skills." He did his best to smile at her.

She smiled back and said, "I've told myself that a thousand times too. They'll be okay. I know they will."

Evan nodded in agreement, and suddenly, the full gravity of the moment fell on him like a boulder. He had felt the woman's pain and believed that she had shared his. Maybe that was the secret to getting through the next year. It seemed to him that sharing things was the secret to succeeding with anything in life.

Rachel made her way back to where Evan sat leaning against a wall. He had been keeping watch on her overstuffed backpack, which carried in it everything possible that Rachel felt she could take with her. The two sat together, knowing they were down to the final few minutes together for quite a long time. Evan took advantage of the moment and started the conversation. "I'm proud of you, you know that, right?"

She grinned broadly and put her head on his shoulder. "Yeah, I know, but it's nice to hear you say it."

"You're going halfway around the world. That's still hard for me to fully comprehend. This is not a weekend drill here at the fort."

"Just remember what I've told you several times," she continued with a confident smile. "No matter how far away I go or no matter where in the world I go, I'll always come back to you."

"I count on that every time you leave me. I'm just waiting for the day you get to come home and actually stay for good."

"I know, but this is just a year. This is just an interruption in our dreams and all the things we've talked about doing. When I get back, we'll get started on them again."

He squeezed her tightly and quietly spoke. "Deal."

Suddenly a voice boomed and called Rachel's unit to formation for a final roll call. She jumped up out of reflex and took her place in one of the lines. The family members there watched silently, lining all the walls of the hangar and realizing the hour of departure had really arrived. As the major bellowed out name after name, Evan could only swallow hard and watch. When Rachel's name was called, she yelled back a loud, strong "Here!" and then gave Evan a smile and a look.

Evan forced a smile in return, but his heart was not in it. Once the roll call was completed, it was announced that the unit would board the plane five minutes later. The group was dismissed from their lines but was instructed not to leave the hangar, giving the soldiers the time for one last quick good-bye with their families. Rachel made her way back to Evan and put her arms around his shoulders for a long, silent, emotional embrace. The two kissed, and Evan repeated his request.

"Please be safe. I want you coming back to me in one piece. We've got a lot of living to do once this is over."

"I'll do my best. I promise," she said as confidently as she could. She strapped on her heavy backpack and waited for their final instructions. She knew it was time to go, and her previously hidden nervousness finally showed as she could not stop fidgeting. Two minutes later, the command was given to board the plane. The final hugs were shared, and the soldiers left the hangar in an impressive line. Each family member watched as long as possible until his specific soldier entered the plane and could no longer be seen. Everyone wanted to draw the process out as long as humanly possible, but the time had come.

Once the plane was full and the doors were closed, Evan went outside and found a spot against the fence to watch the takeoff. The plane's engines drowned out any other sound as it taxied to the end of the runway. It turned around, paused for a moment, and then loudly roared and lunged forward. It sprinted down the runway and left the ground in a matter of seconds. Two minutes later it was a nearly invisible speck in the distant blue sky. Evan turned from the fence and walked slowly to his car. It was all definitely real. His wife, the soldier, was on her way to war.

For Evan, the fifty-mile drive home could easily have been fifty thousand miles, and not even the happiest song on the radio could lighten the heaviness he felt in his heart. He glanced at the sky several times and could see the fragmented white trails left behind by other jets flying people to unknown destinations. Each trail of smoke he saw caused him to relive Rachel's plane disappearing from his view on the horizon. That image had now been forever cemented into his memory, and each mile he drove on the interstate served as a reminder that with each passing minute, Rachel was getting further and further away from him.

She would be gone for a whole year. What would she see and experience during that time? She would be hearing explosions and gunfire while Evan's biggest security concern would be avoiding a rock that might be thrown out of the mower. He worried a lot about how she might change. With every fiber of his being, he wanted the Rachel he had married to be the Rachel who returned to him from Iraq a year from then.

He pulled his car into his driveway and walked to his house. The sun still shined brightly, and his neighborhood was full of life and activity, but when he went inside and closed the door, the outside world disappeared completely, and he was by himself. She had been gone for less than two hours, and he could never remember feeling as alone as he did at that moment, yet he knew that moment was merely the beginning. The part that made him the saddest was that at no time in the past four days had Rachel thought to ask him how he really felt about any of what was happening to them both.

CHAPTER 14

Six hours after Rachel's flight left, Evan went to bed. He wasn't sure why he even tried to sleep because he knew all he would do was toss and turn. She was in the air somewhere over the Atlantic Ocean, which for some would be terrifying by itself, and he knew it would still be several hours before she arrived at her destination. Evan had no idea what route her plane was taking, and he would ask her later just to satisfy his curiosity. He knew the plane would have to land and refuel somewhere, maybe more than once, but he couldn't even guess where that would be. The longest flight he had been on was four hours, and he tried to imagine how tired a person would be after twenty hours on a plane.

Evan lay on his back and stared at his bedroom ceiling. The deployment ceremony had been a touching event filled with both pride and sadness. One thing the day had done was to make Evan very aware that every family in that hangar had its own story. Each had a soldier on that plane just like he did, and he was certain that most of the people he saw there were as restless as he was that first night, mentally swimming or, more accurately, treading water in a sea of uncertainty about the days and months ahead.

Lying alone in bed, he wondered about the impending changes for everyone in that hangar. The upcoming months would surely be the longest periods of separation for most of the spouses involved, and he believed he felt a little better for having talked to that other soldier's wife at the ceremony. He now knew that others felt at least some of the same things he did. Were the others also concerned about the changes in their soldiers after a year in Iraq? Were other spouses lying sleepless in their beds like Evan was? He believed that they had to be equally concerned, but he couldn't know for sure. Evan knew there were family support groups set up for those still at home, but he wondered if those were primarily name-only groups or if they were genuine outlets that would really help. His first thought was that it would be difficult for him or anyone else to open up completely to total strangers even though in theory those strangers would be able to empathize with whatever they heard.

There was so much he had come to realize that he was ill prepared for. He had gone forty-five years basically oblivious to any real specifics regarding the military, and now he had been thrown into the middle of having the army and its decisions affecting his life every single day. He now had army stickers on his car and identification cards in his wallet that gave him privileges on base and in other places, privileges that he never thought would be his to have. He had never sought them out and was certainly unsure how to use them all properly. He would never serve a day in uniform, but he felt every bit as affected by the army as any soldier who had gotten on that plane with Rachel. He would not be carrying an M-16 or wearing a bulletproof vest, but he would be fighting battles of his own on his own. A part of each of his days would now be spent contemplating the worst possible scenarios of a spouse at war. He knew he couldn't escape that, and the best he could do was disguise and mask his true concerns from those he dealt with every day. He felt like he had to put on his happy face for the world no matter how he really felt inside. His eyes finally closed, and he slept while Rachel flew somewhere over the ocean.

Morning number one without her began with a clap of thunder, followed by an August downpour. Evan had thought about golfing, but as he watched the rain through his window, that idea didn't look too promising. He made some coffee and turned on the television to see how long the rain would last. It looked on radar like an isolated storm cell, so Evan thought he still had a chance to get some golf in later in the afternoon. It had been eighteen hours since Rachel's plane had taken off, so she hadn't even landed at her destination yet. Evan tried to guess what country's air space she was flying through at that moment, but he had no real idea. He again looked out the window at his wet yard and a hundred other comfortable, familiar sites, knowing Rachel was soon to enter a totally new world and culture, where everything she saw would be strange, exciting, and potentially deadly.

Evan's phone rang, and when he answered, he heard the cheerful voice of his friend Jordan on the other end. "What are you doing?" began Jordan.

"Nothing much," responded Evan glumly. "What are you up to?"

"Just working on some things in the shop. Come on over if you want."

Evan thought for a second. "Sounds good. I can do that. I'll be over in a few minutes."

"Great," exclaimed Jordan. "See you shortly."

The two lived across town from each other, but visiting Jordan sounded a lot better to Evan than a quiet morning by himself. He filled his coffee cup again, climbed into his car, and drove to his friend's house. Jordan was a hardworking, self-educated, self-employed, good-natured heavy-machine operator. He and Evan had become close friends during the time that Rachel had been away in Guatemala, but he had never actually met her. Jordan only knew her through Evan's words. When Evan pulled up to the shop, he saw Jordan's legs sticking out from underneath a dump truck. Evan always teased his buddy about his big machines and their constant need of attention and repairs, but he never teased seriously because he knew they were Jordan's passion, and every repair gave him purpose. Evan walked into the shop and Evan yelled, "Man, those are some stubby little legs!"

He could hear Jordan laughing from under the truck. "Yeah, yeah," he answered. "I can hear the jealousy in your voice. You just wish you had legs like this."

"Is it that obvious?" laughed Evan.

Jordan came out from under the dump truck, wiped the grease off his hands, and the two visited as the rain played a melody on the tin roof of the shed. Evan took a seat and sipped his coffee, and Jordan sat near him in another plastic chair that was in the shop. Jordan knew some of Evan's thoughts and worries leading up to Rachel's deployment and had anticipated Evan's mood that morning. "So how are you really?" began Jordan. "I thought you might need someone to talk to today."

"Thanks," replied Evan. "I appreciate you calling, and you were right. I wasn't in any mood to sit by myself in the house this morning." Sitting in the shop, Evan temporarily felt a little less alone than before.

Jordan asked about the deployment ceremony and how everything had gone at the base the day before. "So what was it like when she left? I'm sure it was a big deal."

Evan began retelling the events of the day, trying his best to recreate the images and emotions he had experienced. "It was definitely a big thing and pretty impressive. There were several hundred people there doing the same thing I was doing." Jordan listened attentively as Evan continued. "I didn't know what all I would feel once it all got started, but I was really proud of her and sad for her and me at the same time. Everyone there was so excited it looked like a beehive with hundreds of bees buzzing around at the same time."

Jordan laughed at Evan's image choice. "I can only imagine."

"The final formation was quite a deal," continued Evan. "Imagine a whole unit standing at attention, totally silent, and a hangar full of family and friends equally quiet. It was a little eerie, and then suddenly a command was given, and it became a steady stream of soldiers marching out to the plane that would take them off to war. Once they all got onto the plane, it was over. Just like that. After the plane took off, everyone just kind of quietly left."

Evan finished painting the mental picture, and when he was done, Jordan spoke up again. "So how are you feeling? You know I'm not a big emotions guy, but I've been thinking about it and trying to think of what you must be feeling. Are you okay?"

"I'm okay," said Evan with a hint of a smile. "I have to be, and it's not the first time I've been alone with her in another country."

"Well that's true enough."

Evan added, "Besides, it's too early to tell anything. She hasn't even landed there yet."

The downpour eventually turned into a sprinkle, and the gloom gave way to bright sunshine as the storm disappeared. Jordan had, at times, worked on the dump truck while Evan sat and watched. They both knew Evan's limited mechanical abilities, so Jordan only asked him to help with minor things and nothing technical. Evan was hungry and said so. "Hey, let's go get something to eat. I'll buy."

Jordan answered quickly. "I'm in for that, especially if you're buying!" They piled into Evan's car and drove uptown to a restaurant. It was shortly after noon, and the place was crowded with smiling, familiar faces, all busy talking about their issues of the day. There had been an article in the local paper that had featured Rachel and her deployment, so several diners mentioned it to Evan.

He hadn't really thought about others in town taking an interest in his situation, but when he got their questions, he realized how logical their interest was. Every small town in America took pride when one of their own put on the country's uniform and went to war. Evan realized for the first time that others would in part claim a passive ownership in her deployment and that he would be their eyes and ears in order to keep them current on what she was doing in Iraq. He wasn't sure if that would be a good thing or not for the next year. Time would tell, but during that meal alone, Evan was asked about Rachel three different times. Jordan just smiled and ate quietly as Evan told the townspeople what he knew. He quickly developed a standard, stock answer to the questions he received. "As far as, I know she's fine. Thanks for asking." Each person he talked to seemed happy to be in the loop and to vicariously be a part of their local soldier's tour.

The morning rain was long gone and had been replaced by another steamy August afternoon. Evan and Jordan drove back to the shop, and Evan's itch to play golf had returned, so he dropped Jordan off and headed to the course. "You have fun playing with your truck," stated Evan as Jordan got out of his car.

"You know I will," laughed Jordan. "And you have fun with your cow-pasture pool. Thanks for lunch."

Evan shook his head at his friend and drove off, grateful that Jordan had thought enough of him to call and help fill his first morning alone. He headed to the golf course for a few more hours of fun and mental relaxation.

It took four days for Evan to receive any form of communication from Rachel. It took her that long to gain Internet access so that she could let both Evan and her mom know that she had arrived safely and was at her post in Baghdad. The news had come in an e-mail.

Hi, I finally got here to Baghdad, but it took longer than it was supposed to. We had to spend two days in Kuwait waiting for a plane to take all of us the rest of the way in, so that was frustrating. Kuwait was incredibly hot and boring, but now I'm here and ready to get started. I'll let you know more when I can. I haven't even gotten settled in yet.

Love you,
Me

He was relieved she had gotten there safely, but part of him also cringed at the reality of it all. She was really in Iraq in the middle of a war, and he sat at home by his computer completely safe. The two had agreed to stay in touch as often as possible once Rachel knew her schedule. The Internet and instant messenger did their best to reduce the distance, and Evan was thankful to have them. He knew she would let him know as soon as she could when and how often they could talk directly on messenger, but for now, e-mail would have to suffice.

The networking company Evan and Rachel had joined took up the role as Evan's support system while she was gone. He had made many close friends in the company, and he liked the idea that he could lean on them now. He could not remember a luncheon or meeting he had attended while Rachel was in Guatemala where someone had not asked him about her. He knew that would continue now that she was in Iraq, and eight days after Rachel's plane left the fort, he found out that he was right. There was a regional event held, and Evan did what he had done for each such event for the past year—he went by himself. There were several hundred people at the event, many of whom were close friends with Evan. Time after time, he was questioned about Rachel, and each time, he smiled and told the questioner that she had arrived safely in Baghdad. He understood that this extended family had also taken pride and ownership in her deployment just as the townspeople had back home.

The event was productive and educational for Evan, and he had been all smiles for most of the day. He was happy to share his friends' pride in Rachel, and he appreciated their concern for her. Near the end of each regional event, there was always a salute to veterans, and Evan's entire demeanor changed when the slideshow and the music began. Picture after picture of soldiers, flags, and other patriotic images dominated the large screen in the hotel ballroom as Toby Keith's "American Soldier" rang out through the room. Evan stood motionless as he watched and listened, and he lost all control of his emotions when he heard the lines, *"And I don't want to die for you but if dying's asked of me, / I'll bear that cross with honor, 'cause freedom don't come free / I'm an American soldier ..."*

Tears suddenly ran down both cheeks, but he didn't wipe them away. He remained motionless and attentive until the song finished, and then he used his shirt sleeves to try and dry his eyes and face. The tears had greatly surprised him, and he knew he couldn't hide them completely. He had not realized how near the surface his true emotions really were, but now he knew for sure. If Rachel thought she was the only one in the family dealing with a deployment, she was greatly mistaken.

CHAPTER 15

Evan wiped the sand off himself and began to walk the beach. He had gotten thirsty and planned to eventually grab a soda, but first, he just wanted to stretch his legs a while and perhaps dip his toes into the cool gulf water. Laughter and games could be heard and seen along the entire length of the beach. There were still a few hours of daylight left, and Evan saw new arrivals unloading lawn chairs and towels and making their way to the sand. He completely understood their desire to squeeze every possible minute of enjoyment out of the day.

He laughed at himself for walking with just his feet in the water. It was cool, but it wasn't unbearably cold, and it struck him that his beach walk was a metaphor for what his life had become. Four years earlier, he would have been swimming in the water, and now he was content to walk along where it was a few inches deep. There were so many times in the past two years he had disappointed himself. He had watched himself evolve from a swimmer in the ocean of life into a wader content with just dipping a toe into it. He was sure those changes in him had disappointed Rachel too. The scale of their life had gotten far out of balance, and he knew that as she had grown as a soldier, he had begun to lose himself as a husband and even in part as a person. As he threw a shell back into the water, he hoped more answers would reveal themselves to him. That was why he had come to Florida.

After walking the beach for a few more minutes, Evan made his way to a snack shop and bought a Mountain Dew. There were picnic tables nearby, and he found one in the shade in order to get a brief break from the direct sunshine. He sat and relaxed as the other tourists passed him by without giving him a second thought. He had remembered that second beginning with Rachel many times, and he was still amazed at how he could have gone from those smiles that night to the place in which he now found himself. He had once heard a wise man say that everything that had a beginning also had an ending. He had just thought their ending would be much further in the future than it actually turned out to be.

Two months after that dinner with Rachel's family, Evan proposed, and Rachel accepted. He had chosen a ring for her that he liked, spent more than he could afford, and simply asked her if she wouldn't mind spending the rest of her life with him. She had taken about two seconds to tell him that she would love to do that, and shortly after the proposal, Rachel had moved in with him. The wedding invitations were sent from an address they shared, and it seemed to Evan that all that joy was a lifetime ago.

Evan drank the last of his Mountain Dew and enjoyed his temporary shade. He decided to leave his seat and see what souvenirs were offered in the nearest gift shop. The aisles were full of people, who had enthusiasm to spare and money to spend. The shelves were stocked with an enormous variety of trinkets, gadgets, and other unnecessary items, some specific to Fort Myers Beach and other more general things tourists regularly bought. Colorful beach towels were displayed besides goggles and snorkeling gear, and Evan browsed slowly. He had brought a beach towel with him so he skipped those and made his way directly to the hats. Generally, if he ever bought a souvenir for himself, it was a hat, and he saw some that caught his attention. He knew he needed one to protect his head from further sunburn, so he settled on a black one with fancy white lettering that said Fort Myers Beach.

After he bought the hat, he returned to his spot on the beach, determined to soak up the remainder of the beautiful afternoon and equally determined to get closer to sorting out some more of his thoughts. He lay on his stomach and looked around. Before he closed his eyes, he noticed that the pair of college girls had packed up and gone. Apparently they had tanned enough for one afternoon.

A person rarely falls completely asleep lying on a beach, and Evan was no exception. He lay on his stomach with his eyes closed, but memories still raced across his mind, and while the warm sun was relaxing, he knew he would never actually nap. The rhythm of the waves was a soothing complement to the warm sun, and he decided to sit up and give the back sides of his legs a break. They were now completely sunburned and were beginning to ache a bit. Evan sat on his towel with his arms folded across his knees and watched the waves. It was a position he had sat in a hundred times on his front steps while quietly thinking about a host of things. The view of the beach, however, was quite different than what he was used to seeing in his front yard.

Evan had grown so tired of feeling empty and listless and lost. He mentally turned back the clock and thought of all he had in his life four years earlier that was no longer his. Sometimes he wondered how and why he even got out of bed now. The stack of things that had vanished from his life was substantial, and Evan realized that he basically had two choices. He could either give up or fight to get some of those things back. He had come to understand that he was sitting on that beach in order to reach that decision. He was reminded of Robert Frost's poem "The Road Not Taken" and was now fully able to appreciate its significance.

The afternoon sun began to fall into the horizon, and people started to pack up and leave for other places. Evan remained a while longer, and he just sat and quietly watched the waves and the seagulls. He was still invisible and anonymous, and after all his thinking, suddenly neither of those qualities appealed to him like they had before, and he decided he was ready to be noticed and included in the world again. He had always been easily moved by the ordinary daily miracles of life—an emotional song, a child's joy, or a moving end to a movie—but he knew his heart had been somewhat hardened the past couple years. He hadn't felt any real emotions for several months, and on this Florida trip, he had been searching for his old self, and he wondered silently if he was on a fool's mission. He hoped not.

He watched couples walking hand in hand along the shore, simply sharing the experience with each other, and he thought moments like that were now gone from his future. He desperately wanted to again be able to cherish life's simple joys and have someone special to share them with, but he did not know where to find the key that unlocked that door for him. He had never imagined that door would ever close for him but he felt like it had.

Without warning, the clouds began to overtake the previously sunny beach. The couples and families he had watched enjoying the day had reinforced to him that his destiny now seemed to be one of a solitary figure, who may not again get to share those simple yet magical moments with a loved one. He had thought about that before but had never allowed the thought to stay in his mind for long because it scared him. He had no desire to grow old alone, but now he faced that potential reality head on. He realized no one's destiny was totally written ahead of time and, that as long as he had breath, he could choose another path. He also knew that a huge part of his current frustration had come from the fact that so much of what had happened in the past three years had been out of his control. For someone with his mentality, feeling helpless to manage his own life was a difficult pill to swallow.

The night before he flew to Florida, he had watched his favorite movie, *Forrest Gump*, and though he had watched the movie many times, this time he put himself into the movie in a very different way. It dawned on him as he watched Forrest looking out over his balcony and staring blankly from his porch that, in many ways, that had been him. Forrest waited patiently for his Jenny while she explored the world without him. His life, though he lived day to day by himself, was always filled with the belief that Jenny would return and be with him. He never lost hope and never doubted they would be together, and the times he spent with her were the best moments of his life.

Evan couldn't help noticing the similarities between that and what he had lived while Rachel had been away in uniform. He felt very much like Forrest, his life floating around on a breeze, not seeing or understanding his purpose. Being alone had never been fulfilling to him in any way because both Evan and Forrest knew there was more.

Forrest waited until Jenny eventually made her way back to where she had begun her journey. She had been lost for much of that time but had finally grown and had seen what was really important in life. Rachel seemingly had been lost and restless in ways Evan had never guessed, and on her journey with the military, she had grown and had apparently found herself once she put on her uniform and left America's borders. Even though she had promised Evan that she would always return to him, the lure of distant, exotic places had shown itself to be too big a draw to resist. He wondered if the sweet smell of the trimmed grass of home could ever again match the allure of an Iraqi dust storm.

The late afternoon clouds grew thicker and darker over the Florida beach, and Evan decided he had sat in the sand long enough. He shook out his towel, draped it over his shoulder, and ambled back to his car. He put the roof up and drove slowly back to his hotel. It would not be dark for over an hour yet, so Evan grabbed a beer from his refrigerator and went to sit on his deck. His skin wore the results of his day in the sun, but the Fort Myers heat still felt good to him. The day had been full of reflection time for which he was pleased with himself. For him, this trip was about cleaning out his mental cupboards and sorting out memories and emotions that had remained pent up for far too long. The process had been engaged and undertaken, and once the cork was off the bottle, they had all begun flowing much more freely than they ever had at home.

The sky still suggested a storm, but no rain had started, so Evan kicked back in his chair and watched the flurry of activity below him on the street. The sight of palm trees lining roads was still new and exciting to him. Throughout his life, he had watched maple and elm trees change with the seasons, so the palm trees made him feel warm, especially on this winter trip. He saw a couple walking together, holding hands. They were in their fifties and appeared unmoved by the ominous sky. They seemed to be far more focused on each other, and Evan watched them as long as he could. They smiled and laughed with each step they took, and their arms swung high together back and forth as one. Nothing seemed to matter to either of them except the person each held onto. Evan had known how incredible that feeling was, and watching others that much in love pained him far more than he had ever admitted to anyone. He missed that and wanted those feelings back.

The couple walked around the corner and out of sight, and Evan was again alone with his beer and his thoughts. His mind took him to the last time he could remember walking and laughing like the couple he had just seen. It was two and a half years earlier in New Orleans, and he mentally revisited what had turned out to be one of his favorite weekends with Rachel. No matter what all had happened since then, whenever Evan remembered that trip, he still found a smile.

Their networking company was having a national convention on the Riverfront there. Evan had never been to New Orleans, and Rachel wanted to see the city again to see how much everything there had improved in the year since her Guard trip there to clean up the Hurricane Katrina mess. The convention ran from a Thursday afternoon until the gala banquet concluded on Saturday night. The two had left Wednesday afternoon and had driven until 1:30 AM and then decided to stop at a hotel in Mississippi, an hour north of New Orleans, and catch a few hours of sleep. They were up early and were driving along Poydras Street in front of the Super Dome before 10:00 Thursday morning.

As Evan and Rachel checked into the Hilton, other teammates greeted them, and the festivities got underway early. The couple found their room and then went outside to explore the New Orleans Riverfront area. It was a beautiful September day, and this area showed no signs of ever enduring a hurricane. Harrah's was right across the street from the Hilton, and Bourbon Street was within walking distance, so there was plenty to do when the convention was not in session.

The first meeting was that afternoon and Evan and Rachel were enthused to learn business building tips and techniques from the company's leaders. Evan took several pages of notes during the session and was happy to again see teammates from all over the country, ones he didn't get to see often enough. He had been to a convention before, but he had gone alone, and he was extremely happy to have Rachel with him this time. Rachel and Evan had reached the first major level of achievement in the company and got to cross the big stage to be recognized in front of all those attending the event. It was exhilarating for both of them to hear their names called in front of over three thousand people and to be singled out at the team meeting. It was all so much more special for Evan because Rachel was there to share it all with him.

The next two days were filled with learning sessions, great meals, and sightseeing. Harrah's had been a regular stop for Evan during breaks, and he was over $300 ahead after some good luck on the slot machines. They had also joined some teammates and had walked to Bourbon Street twice. Walking hand in hand, the romance of the French Quarter worked its magic on both of them.

"This street is so cool," remarked Evan as they walked.

"Yeah it is," smiled Rachel. "There is nothing quite like it."

He squeezed her hand tightly. "I'm really glad you are here with me. This wouldn't be half as fun by myself."

"I'm glad too. I'm having a great time."

They popped in and out of several of the bars and shared laughter and dances like they had not done since their wedding day. To Evan, it felt like a four-day-long date, and he savored it all. The icing on the cake was the gala banquet Saturday night, a dinner and dance that brought the convention to a close. Rachel looked beautiful in her formal dress, and Evan felt incredibly proud to know she was with him. They danced at least a dozen fast songs and held each other tightly during the slow ones. The rest of the world disappeared for Evan as he lost himself in Rachel's warmth and beauty. He even remembered a very special song

the band had played that night, and it had meant so much to him that
he memorized the lyrics. It was a Sara Evans song that he knew would
stick in his memory forever.

Lying here with you, listening to the rain
Smiling just to see the smile upon your face,
These are the moments I thank God that I'm alive,
These are the moments I remember all my life,
I've found all I've waited for, and I could not ask for more.

Looking in your eyes, seeing all I need,
Everything you are is everything in me,
These are the moments I know heaven must exist,
These are the moments I know all I need is this,
I've found all I've waited for, and I could not ask for more.

I could not ask for more than this time together,
I could not ask for more than this time with you,
Every prayer has been answered
Every dream I've had has come true,
Right here in this moment is right where I'm meant to be,
Here with you here with me ...

Everything was new and wonderful for him again, at least for that
weekend. There was no way Evan could have imagined that he and
Rachel would never again get the chance to share another weekend
like that one. Even the long drive home was enjoyable to him, for when
he looked over at Rachel sleeping in the passenger seat, he saw that she
wore a peaceful smile that warmed his entire soul.

Evan had gotten so lost in his memories of New Orleans that it
took a huge clap of thunder before he even realized that it had begun
raining. The early evening was still warm, and Evan didn't mind the
cool raindrops sharing his deck with him for a little while. When he

finished his beer, he decided to get out of his swimsuit and get dressed to go out and eat.

The Sand Crabbe had been enjoyable the night before, so Evan decided to return. The parking lot was mostly full, but Evan found a spot and dodged raindrops on his way to the door. The music was a pleasant greeting for him, and he claimed a stool at the bar just a few seats away from where he had sat and talked with Tony the night before. Evan was again grateful for having met someone with similar experiences and worries as his own, and he sincerely hoped that Tony would return home to a long and happy life with his wife and children.

Evan ordered the biggest cheeseburger on the Sand Crabbe's menu, along with a Michelob and then settled in. He planned to be there for a while. Perhaps it was because it was a Saturday night. Perhaps it was because of the rain that limited outdoor activities. Whatever it was, the Sand Crabbe was full of both tourists and locals enjoying themselves. Once Evan finished his burger, he turned his stool around and became part of the evening's fun. His toes tapped to "Celebration," and he watched the dance floor fill up. He could see the steady rainfall through the bar's windows, and that was the only dark aspect of the night. It was not enough to dampen anyone's mood inside the club, however, and Evan was still happy to trade the snow and ice of home for a warm rain in Florida.

CHAPTER 16

For Evan, days had become longer than twenty-four hours. He checked his e-mail at least a dozen times each day and found himself watching CNN and other news shows more often than he had ever done before. Every tidbit of information that dealt with Baghdad got his attention, and he sought out every glimpse of Iraq footage he could see just in case Rachel was in one of the camera shots.

In less than a month, Rachel made her situation sound routine and almost mundane, but Evan didn't trust her casual words. He saw no way that day-to-day life in Baghdad could be low-key, and even though her e-mails made her sound safe and relaxed, he doubted he ever was told the whole story of her life there. He had asked himself many times whether it was better to hear the whole truth or be pacified and kept partially in the dark, but he could never decide for sure.

Summer nights at home gave way to harvest moons, and as the days got shorter, Evan's solitary nights grew even longer and colder. He was a full-time networker now and felt some pressure to build the business he and Rachel had begun. When they had started the business, their shared goals and efforts were exciting. They had been a team, and each had seen the business as something they could always share and build together, but outside forces had wedged their way between some of those goals and priorities. Evan had always seen the possibilities of the business and how it could positively change their lives, and he certainly enjoyed spending time with his teammates, but with Rachel gone so much and with her growing disinterest in working the business with him, he found his motivation waning. It didn't take long for him to reach the conclusion that for the most part, he was going through the motions and not really working it like he knew he should. The business became just another pond for Evan to dip his toes into.

Six weeks into Rachel's deployment, Evan had another birthday, and other than a call from his parents, the day went unnoticed by everyone else. Evan checked his e-mail many times that day, hoping for a message from his wife, but it never came. He had already grown frustrated with not being able to share Rachel's birthdays, their anniversaries, and other important days with her, and that frustration grew when she missed his birthday for the second time. When his day ended, the smile he should have worn was replaced with an apathetic frown. It wasn't long before the toe dipping he was doing in their networking business spilled over to other parts of his life as well. The following night, there was an e-mail waiting for him. He read it a couple times and then went to the living room to watch the news.

Hi, Sorry I'm a day late with this but Happy Birthday! Sometimes I forget the time difference, and it gets me messed up with things at home. Hope you had a great day. Everything is fine here, and I'm keeping busy. Still hotter than hell!

Love you,
Me

He tried to be happy that at least she wasn't so absorbed in her own things that she had totally forgotten, but he still felt the sting of disappointment from the day before. An e-mail the next day couldn't totally cure that, especially when he remembered that Baghdad time was eight hours ahead of home, not behind, so in reality she had missed his birthday by two days, not one.

Thanksgiving arrived, and Evan was invited to share the day with Rachel's mom and brothers. He welcomed the invitation and looked forward to not having to spend the holiday alone. Rachel's mom and sister-in-law had cooked all morning, and there was more food there than could be eaten by the ten people. It was an excellent meal followed by a relaxing afternoon watching football, and Evan found himself nodding off from time to time on the couch. During the second NFL game, the telephone rang. Rachel's mom answered it, and her face immediately glowed.

Rachel was on the other end of the line. Evan later learned that Rachel and her mom had worked out the time of the call through e-mail messages, and after a short private talk, Rachel's brothers, the kids, and Evan all got to speak with her as well. She had bought an international phone and had loaded it with a lot of minutes. The conversations were light and lively and short enough so that each person could have a turn, and everyone was glad to hear her voice. It was the kids' turns first.

"Hey, how hot is it there?" asked a niece.

"Hi Aunt Rachel. We just ate a lot. How are you?"

"Are you shooting your gun a lot?"

Then her brothers said a quick hello, followed by their wives and then Rachel's mom. Evan took the phone last and tried his best to get caught up with his wife's activities as the audience in the room pretended to be disinterested. It was basically a time for her to reassure those closest to her that she was well and safe, and Evan knew he and Rachel would talk again soon without the others nearby.

"Hi. It's great to hear your voice," beamed Evan. "We missed you today, but then I miss you every day, so I can't really tell the difference from one day to the next. You sound good."

"Good to hear you too," answered Rachel. "It sounds like everyone is having a big day there."

"Yeah, it's been fun and relaxing, and the food was great. Did you get some kind of Thanksgiving meal there?"

"Actually, we did. Our congressman was here for a couple days, so everybody from our state got a special Thanksgiving meal with him, which was kind of cool."

"Excellent," stated Evan. "I wondered what they would do for all of you during the holidays."

"It wasn't the same as a meal at home, but it was pretty good. I'd better get back to work. Give everyone there another hug for me, and I'll talk to you soon."

"Will do," smiled Evan. "Be careful. Thanks for calling. I love you."

"Bye."

After the call, the family all showed a lot more energy, and thoughts of naps were quickly forgotten. The next fifteen minutes was spent discussing how good she sounded and how pleased everyone was to have gotten to talk with her. Her mom could not wipe the grin off her face and apparently had no real desire to try. For this one night, she had a chance to sleep more restfully than usual because for the moment, she knew that Rachel was safe. She would worry about tomorrow when tomorrow arrived.

Evan also breathed a bit easier and was grateful Rachel and her mom had worked out the time for Rachel to call. It had been a very nice surprise. Anytime he could hear his wife's voice and know that she was all right, it made the day better. An hour after the call, Evan thanked everyone and then headed home. It had been as good a holiday as possible without Rachel there to share it with him.

Lying in bed that night, Evan felt an odd combination of joy, pride, and loneliness. He had been happy to talk to Rachel and was glad she was safe for that day, but his nights had become mentally troublesome for him, and her phone call could not help him escape that. The quiet times at home and the thinking time in bed were not his friends, and his mind wandered often to all the potential negatives of her situation and how one unknown person in a faraway land could change every plan he and Rachel had ever made together. He knew his feelings had been multiplied and intensified because that day was a holiday, and before he drifted off to sleep, he thought ahead to Christmas and anticipated that it would be even more difficult to be alone then.

He had been right. The entire Christmas season was as dismal for Evan as he had thought it would be, and far too often, he felt like a Scrooge. There was snow on the ground, decorations on the neighborhood houses, and carols on the radio, but none of those things could provide any inner glow for him as each day served as a reminder of another holiday spent without his wife. He had listened to Earl Nightingale's "The Strangest Secret" many times and understood that people become what they think about the most, and he wondered if he had created a self-fulfilling prophecy of Christmas gloom for himself. He knew it was entirely possible. Rachel loved the Christmas season, and Evan had always worked hard to find a special, unique gift for her.

One year, he even started his search for the perfect Christmas gift in early August. He got online and began looking for a way to bring one of Rachel's dreams to life. She was a huge Brett Favre and Green Bay Packers fan, and Favre had convinced America he was about to retire, so Evan's creativity kicked into high gear. He searched eBay for tickets to the Bears-Packers Christmas Day game at Lambeau Field, and he found a pair he could afford. On Christmas Eve, the two boarded a plane and flew to Green Bay for the game. The trip had been even better than he had imagined it would be, and Evan had been very happy with his gift to her. If she had told him more of her dreams, he would have worked equally hard to make them come to life for her, but when she was in Iraq, the best he could do for Christmas was pack a box with flavored coffee, snacks, a couple paperbacks, and a loving, romantic card. He felt incredibly cheated.

Rachel called twice during December, and she and Evan talked for about half an hour each time. Evan was always full of questions, wanting to know what things she was seeing, doing, and feeling in Iraq. Rachel told him what she could without crossing the lines of classified material, and Evan did his best to try and mentally picture the things she relayed to him.

"So tell me what all you've been doing," began Evan.

"Just working mostly. It doesn't take long for anything to become routine, even here. I did get to do one cool thing though. We all have to take turns on guard duty at one of the palaces here, and you wouldn't believe that place. I took lots of pictures, and I'll send them to you. Talk about living big!"

"I can't wait to see them. I'm guessing the weather is better there now than when you got there."

"A lot better, but it gets cold here too, especially at night. You know how deserts are when the sun goes down. It can go from eighty-five degrees to forty pretty fast."

"There are a lot of days here now that I'd love to see forty degrees!"

"I understand," replied Rachel. "I don't miss anything about winter at home. That's for sure."

"Anything else exciting going on for you there?"

"Well, I got to ride in an Apache helicopter, which was amazing. A group of us had to go to an outlying camp for a day, so I got to see some of the countryside instead of just the camp here."

"You mean you were out where it was easier for people to shoot at you?"

"I guess so, but I'm fine. It was exciting. Oh, and we had a huge dust storm the other day. I have pictures of that too that I'll send you. I couldn't see anything, and the damn dust gets into everything here—the food, my clothes, everything."

"That doesn't sound like fun. No dust storms back here. Just a little snow and ice."

"You can keep that there. Well, I'd better get going. I'll save some of the minutes on my phone and call you again before long."

"Okay," answered Evan softly. "Be careful, especially if you take more helicopter rides. I miss you."

"Bye," replied Rachel.

It usually took just a couple minutes for Evan to get her caught up on things at home, if she even asked about them, for like in most small towns, things rarely changed. It was always good to hear her voice, but at the same time, the calls were just a temporary relief for his loneliness, and just like at Thanksgiving, Evan's worries were allayed for a day. He knew that the day after each call from her, he would worry again. Every moment for her in Baghdad brought with it the chance for missiles to come over the wall of the compound, and Evan could never shake his concerns completely.

In early December, Evan put up his Christmas tree in their living room, more for symbolic reasons than anything else. He thought that if he saw the tree lit up, it might brighten his spirits. At times it worked, but overall, Evan remained blue as the calendar inched closer to Christmas. He felt hypocritical at festive gatherings, but he pasted on smiles and cheers and told countless concerned people that Rachel was fine and that he heard from her often. There were dozens of networking friends who had never met Rachel but who thought enough of Evan to be concerned for her. They viewed her as an extension of their family and took some form of personal pride in knowing that one of their own was serving in the war on their behalf. As it turned out, they would never meet Rachel, for she would never fully grasp the level of esteem for which they held her, and this group of people, despite their care and sincerity, were apparently viewed as an extra unwanted obligation to Rachel. When she finally returned home for good, she had several chances to meet and thank the group for their thoughts and prayers and good wishes, but instead, she found excuses and reasons to be elsewhere whenever there was a gathering or an event. Evan could never figure out why she had done that, and he always did his best to make excuses for her and to make her look good in their eyes. Eventually, he ran out of excuses and quit trying.

Christmas Eve arrived, accompanied by a silent, gentle snow shower. Evan turned on his Christmas tree lights and watched his front yard turn white. He knew that all over America, families were gathering, meals were being shared, and children's eyes were wide with eager anticipation of gifts yet unwrapped; and he tried his best to smile for their joy. He knew his Christmas would once again be much different than any of those.

Evan's Christmas highlight was a large cheeseburger and a baked potato, followed by his annual viewing of *It's a Wonderful Life* on television. This time, he found himself more immersed in George Bailey's character than usual. Every time George stayed home so that someone else could chase a dream, he cringed a bit. Evan could readily identify with being the one left at home, and he could completely empathize with George's frustration in the movie when he kicked his car door and watched his rich friend Sam head to Florida for a vacation.

Evan could only hope that his Clarence would soon arrive to show him that his time at home was not futile and that his life still had a purpose. He sat alone and pondered whether or not a large group would show up for him if he became $8,000 short in his life. His biggest unanswered question was what Rachel would do to put her own goals aside if he really needed her to be there for him. As he watched Mary beam with pride in her husband at the end of the movie, Evan wondered if Rachel could pinpoint the day when her pride in him had faded to the point of no return.

The movie ended, and as he always did, Evan wiped the tears from his cheeks and smiled. The goodness of the characters always moved him emotionally, and the message that one good person can change the world was never lost on him. Evan knew that for most of his adult life, he had been a shadow of George Bailey, helping others through his teaching and coaching, but while Rachel was gone, he felt much more like the lost, frustrated George—and there was no Clarence in sight to show him otherwise.

Evan did not wait up for Santa. He watched the news after the movie ended and then went to bed. Rachel was eight hours ahead of him, so Christmas morning was arriving in Baghdad as he was heading to bed. As he lay in bed staring blankly at the ceiling, he thought of Rachel and her Christmas breakfast in a war zone. He assumed the army would do something special to celebrate the day with the thousands of soldiers so far from their families, and as he tried to picture Rachel's morning, he hoped that she was missing him like he was missing her. No celebration of any kind was ever as good as it could be if you have no one special to share it with. He had learned that lesson very well over the past year and a half, and this Christmas had reinforced the lesson in a big way. It was the loneliest Christmas Eve he could ever remember.

Christmas Day began with coffee and some heartwarming stories on the morning news. The yard was still covered with snow, and Evan smiled as he mentally compared his morning to Rachel's day in the desert. He poured his second cup of coffee and thought ahead to New Year's Eve, and even though it was a week away, he was already not looking forward to it.

CHAPTER 17

Evan had been correct. New Year's Eve was every bit as bleak for him as Christmas had been, and he spent it alone at home. He rarely went out on New Year's Eve anyway, preferring to stay off the roads, and this year that decision had been very easy for him. Like many days that could have been special, it had turned into just another ordinary day. For quite some time, he had felt like he was losing his way and losing himself, and the holiday season had served to amplify each feeling of insecurity that swirled inside him. He had grown to realize the true importance of having a purpose in life because without one, what he mostly felt was lost. He was extremely happy to see the entire holiday season come to an end because throughout the holidays, he had begun to feel like a ship adrift on the sea without anyone manning the helm. The ship could drift aimlessly for days and weeks heading nowhere, not caring or having any control over which direction the wind blew it, and he knew that was no way to live. He could never grasp why Rachel had not allowed him to share in holding the wheel of the ship they had promised to share at their wedding, and it seemed to him that at times she almost enjoyed the futility he felt, and that hurt him a lot. With each message and conversation, it seemed to Evan that she conveyed just enough superiority to him that it made him feel bad. He wondered many times what she must have felt she gained by doing that, but he could never totally figure it out. He could only think that daily military behavior and attitudes had begun to permanently rub off on her, and with each day, he lost a little more hope of ever getting back the woman he had married.

January was as ordinary and uneventful for Evan as November and December had been, and the cold and darkness of winter did nothing to raise his spirits. Rachel's almost daily e-mails had dwindled to a couple of short greetings each week, and each time she wrote about how busy she was and told of all the new and exciting things she was experiencing without every really going into detail. As he read them, he felt further and further apart from her because he could not identify with any of what she told him, and she did little to help him with that in any way. There was nothing new and exciting on his end, and he could feel the ship of his life drifting further off course.

The first week of February shattered Evan's mundane routine and gave him a temporary purpose he would have rather not had. The entire area where he lived got caught up in a hellish two-day ice storm that left its mark on every fence, tree, road, and home within a seventy-mile radius of Evan's home. Tree limbs snapped like kindling, and neighborhoods sounded like war zones as tree after tree was either killed or forever altered by the weight of the ice. Temperatures were frigid, and tens of thousands of people were out of power for as long as three weeks. As bad as the ice storm was, the thaw out was nearly as destructive. Evan and Rachel had finished the basement of their dreams in their house, and it was full of many of their most valuable things. One corner had a couch, a big screen television, and several chairs. Next to that area was a section filled with four full-sized arcade games. There was an eight-foot pool table in the center of the basement, and on the other side of that there was a workout area, complete with a weight bench and a Bowflex. The last section contained shelves that held the hundreds of books the two had collected and read over the years. There was also a seven-foot long oval table with six chairs, along with a stereo so anyone enjoying the basement could also listen to music. In all there was over $15,000 worth of prized possessions in the basement, and Evan spent a great deal of his time down there.

It seemed to begin all at once, though when Evan looked back on it, he knew that wasn't true. Four days after the ice storm hit the area, the temperature began to slowly rise. The basement had never had any water in it since Evan and Rachel had moved in, so he was totally caught off guard when he walked down the steps and saw a lake covering the entire floor. His heart sank as he took in the scene, and his mind filled with more hopelessness, helplessness, and frustration. He knew he had a lot of work ahead, but he had no idea just how much work it would really be. He really didn't know where to begin, but he knew he had to do something and do it quickly. He and Rachel owned a small wet vac, so he ran to the garage and brought it to the basement. The water was over his shoes as he hurried to the outlet to plug the wet vac in. He turned the machine on, and in just a few seconds, it was full and ready to be emptied. Since there was nowhere to dump the water in the basement, Evan had to carry it all upstairs and pour it into the kitchen sink.

He repeated that process a dozen times and then realized it was a lost cause. It would take weeks to empty the basement doing it that way, and the water needed to be drained far more quickly than that. His current plan would also wear him out long before he even made a dent in the water level, so he decided to drive to a hardware store and buy a submergible sump pump. He hooked it up, placed it in the middle of the basement floor, and ran a garden hose out to the middle of his icy backyard. The water began to slowly drain, but Evan's real work had just begun.

Before the water level in the basement had noticeably changed, Evan began the long process of saving their valuables. The job of carrying things upstairs and drying out what could be dried appeared quite daunting, but he didn't want things to be completely ruined, and he knew he had to get them out of the water as fast as he could. He started with the twenty plastic storage tubs stacked on the floor and then went to the books that were stored on the bottom shelves of the bookcases. The couch was ruined, and he could only hope the big screen TV and the arcade games were not soaked beyond repair. The sump pump motor serenaded each trip up and down the stairs that Evan made. He could not immediately know how many of their things could not be saved and would have to be discarded. He would have to wait at least a full day and get everything dry before he could even begin to get a handle on the damage.

On approximately his eightieth trip up and down the basement stairs, Evan began thinking of Rachel. He wished she had been there to help him, and he got more frustrated as the thought continued to linger in his mind. All he could do was tell her in an e-mail what had happened and what he was going through even though she couldn't do anything about it from halfway around the world. She wasn't at home. She was never at home. For the next fifteen days, Evan spent most of his waking hours in the basement hating his wet vac and resenting Rachel's eagerness to be elsewhere.

Evan's thoughts were confirmed after he sent Rachel an e-mail telling her part of the situation at home. He typed enough for her to get the general picture, but he knew she would never comprehend all the specifics of the hundreds of hours he had spent trying to save their house and their belongings.

Hi, I've had a hell of a time here. Don't know if you heard or not but the whole area had a wicked ice storm. It wiped out nearly every tree, and houses were torn up. Power is still out all over the place. Our basement flooded big time, and I'm working on getting everything out of there to somewhere dry upstairs. The sump pump has been working nonstop and is making a difference, but it's still a big mess. Not having much fun to say the least! Hope everything is good on your end.

Me

She had her own duties on base to worry about, and her reply had been relatively brief.

Hey, Sorry to hear about the ice mess. I bet you are sick of the water already. I'm sure you'll get it all taken care of. I've been busy here with my work, but there's not much to do on my off hours. Some of us have been working out at the gym, and I like doing that. Otherwise, it's pretty much the same routine. Good luck with everything.

Me

For many of the fifteen days following the basement flood, Evan felt like he was just spinning his wheels. He would vacuum up a wet area, move to another and then another, and the water would be gone for a while. An hour later, it was as if he had never been there at all, and the process was repeated. Evan understood how quickly a damp basement could turn to mold and mildew, so he continued to do everything he had to do in order to get the water completely out. He had no choice but to do that, but at least, for a while, he felt like he had a purpose.

Once Evan e-mailed Rachel that the initial flood was under control, she rarely inquired about it again, and Evan could never figure that out. It was her house too, and a lot of her things had gotten wet or ruined. Did none of that matter to her anymore? Her lack of curiosity and interest in even major things at home bewildered him. She evidently assumed that whatever happened at home was not as interesting or as important to her as what she did in Baghdad, so she simply didn't ask about them. Once Evan came to understand the unwritten rules of their conversations and e-mails, he decided that he would only tell her about home if something really major occurred. He became painfully aware that if it didn't involve something military, a topic would probably not hold her interest for long. He gave up trying to compete for her interest and attention and became something he had never been before—a man without a purpose or a goal to shoot for, and he already hated what he had begun to evolve into. He knew his sail was down, and the boat of his life was simply drifting aimlessly. He hoped he could find the energy to once again raise the sail and chart a productive course to travel.

Eventually, the basement dried out, but to Evan, it had seemed it would never happen. Every day, there were puddles to get rid of, only to have them return a short time later. Outside, the remnants of the ice storm were everywhere, and Evan knew they would be seen and felt for months, if not years to come. Even the smallest drizzle would again create multiple puddles of water that demanded Evan's attention, and he eventually lost track of the number of hours he was forced to spend in the basement. He only knew there were way too many for his liking, and each day, he resented more and more having to deal with all it by himself.

CHAPTER 18

Evan's feet tapped even faster as the band at the Sand Crabbe went into their version of "Free Ride." The partiers on the dance floor responded with arms raised and a chorus of cheers, and even though Evan was suddenly in the mood to join them, he remained on his stool. He looked around the bar for a potential dance partner, and he was surprised how foreign it felt to look for a woman to be with other than Rachel, even if it was just for a dance. When Evan held Rachel for the first time several years earlier, he was sure she would be the last first kiss of his life. He didn't really believe in the concept of soul mates, but if there were such a thing, he could have easily been convinced that she was his. She was a bit shy then, very self-conscious and insecure, but he knew her heart was right, and he could see early on in their relationship that she would give or do anything for those special few in her world. He had wanted very much to be one of those people for a long, long time.

As he watched the crowd, Evan wondered if any of the couples there were on their first date together, and if so, were any of them already thinking that a life partner had been found? "Free Ride" wound down, and the group slowed the music down so the couples could get close. He watched the smiles and the embraces for a moment and then turned his stool back around to face the bar. A war of nerves rushed through his body and surprised him. In his heart, he knew the day would come when he might find someone else to be with, and if he had thought he was ready, the response of his body had told him that he might not be. When he realized what he was feeling, a silent anger directed toward Rachel grew inside him. At that moment, in his mind, everything had been her fault, but a few seconds later, he calmed down. They both had a role in what had happened to them, and he knew he had to get over thoughts like that and move on.

A young couple walked behind him, and though he didn't hear the entire conversation, he heard the woman giggle and say, "I promise." He was tempted to turn around and tell the young man not to believe her but he refrained. He instantly thought back to some of the promises that Rachel had made and broken, and he just shook his head. He knew this weekend was all about attempting to come to terms with those broken promises and shattered dreams and the fact that they were now gone. He had never truly vented his real inner feelings to anyone, even though at times he felt as if he might explode. He had talked several times with Jordan about some of his frustration but had never totally opened up about everything to anyone.

More than anything else he could think of, he hated the idea of growing old alone. It terrified him, and when he met Rachel, he had believed that worry had vanished for him. He had relished that feeling and that security, so as he sat by himself on a stool at the Sand Crabbe in Fort Myers, Florida, his frustration toward Rachel and her choices strengthened. He thought to himself that perhaps it was time all his feelings found their way to the surface. They had been withheld long enough. He even had a fleeting thought of starting a fight with someone just for the hell of it, but that idea quickly left his mind. That wasn't his way, and he knew it.

The tempo of the music picked up once again, and the party was on. Evan finished his beer and ordered another one. While the band played "China Grove," Evan's cell phone rang. He grabbed his beer, answered the phone, and walked to what he thought was the quietest section of the bar. He smiled when he heard Jordan's friendly voice on the other end.

"What the hell are you up to?" began Jordan. "It sounds loud there. What are you doing? Partying?"

Evan laughed. "Of course I am. You didn't think I came here to just sit on my butt, did you?"

"Well, are you getting anything figured out, or did you hit the beach and forget why you went down there?"

Jordan was always so straightforward and blunt. He rarely minced words and usually said what he was thinking without any sugarcoating. It was one of the things Evan liked most about his friend. The others included his loyalty, his honesty, and his incredibly high character.

"I haven't forgotten why I came here." Evan spoke loudly so that he could be heard over the band and the crowd. "The weather here has been awesome, and I've gotten a chance to do a lot of thinking. Whether or not I've figured anything out is still up for grabs, but I think I'm on my way to doing that."

"That's good," continued Jordan. "All you've missed here at home is a really cold weekend. I wish I was there with you. Warm sounds pretty good." Jordan had understood Evan's need to get away and at least try and clear his head, and while both men knew that two days might not be long enough to heal an internal would, it could be the first important step on the road to doing that. There would always be more to think about and decide. "I just wanted to check up on you and make sure some alligator hadn't eaten you or something. Get on back to your music and have a great time. I'll see you when you get back."

"Okay," stated Evan with a grin. "Hey, thanks for calling. I appreciate it. See you soon."

"You bet. Be good," concluded Jordan.

Evan finished his talk with Jordan and rejoined the party. He took a long drink from his beer bottle and looked for a seat. His stool had been taken by someone else, but he saw a table that was coming open as a couple prepared to leave for the night. Evan didn't hesitate and immediately went to claim the spot. While he sat and listened to the music, he thought more about his flooded basement, golf games, networking, and other aspects of life at home. He realized that none of those things matched up well when compared with helicopter rides, M-16s, Kevlar vests, and salutes. It was easy for him to see how he and Rachel had drifted apart, but he wanted to know when she had actually decided that whatever feelings she once had for him were irrevocably gone. He had tried to be interested in her military activities, but he had never fully been able to get into the inner circle of that part of her world.

All the training, the drills, the protocols, and the military routines had always been foreign to him, and there was nothing he could ever do about it. The joy and excitement Rachel always showed when she prepared for any army trip had always been bittersweet for Evan. He was proud of her, but he was equally puzzled by her disinterest in trying to help him understand why she couldn't muster the same enthusiasm for being home with him. He had come to realize that he would never know the answer to that question. He had also come to understand that she would never fully grasp his frustration level as he went from having the dream of a life with her to spending 80 percent of their marriage alone while she changed priorities and personalities in other countries and causally left him and their marriage behind. To Evan, the worst part of all of it was that he could not remember a single time when she had asked him how he felt about what was happening to them. He could only surmise that either she didn't really care how he felt or that she believed avoiding the answer had been easier than facing it.

Evan's table was closer to the band and the dance floor than his stool had been, and he started to feel more a part of the evening's fun than he had earlier. The music was loud and energizing to him, and he realized just how long it had been since he had allowed himself to go out and cut loose. He mused that if he were to look into a mirror, he might, for the first time in a very long time, recognize the face looking back at him. That revelation also made him sad to think about the incredible amount of wasted time he had endured.

Month after month, losing a piece of one's identity can leave some deep marks on a person's psyche. Evan knew he was not the same person he had been three years earlier, and he took responsibility for that because he knew life was a series of daily choices no matter what hand he was dealt. The personal growth material from his networking business had taught him that, so he couldn't really blame Rachel for all that he had become. She had a hand in the process for sure, but in the end, he knew that he had chosen to withdraw from the world, to retreat instead of charge, to procrastinate instead of act, and to accept the defeat of the biggest part of his life instead of fighting like hell to keep it. He knew his trip to Florida was the starting block for his next life chapter, and his most prevailing thought now was wondering how long he would have to run this race by himself. Evan wanted to tell someone, anyone, that whoever thought only the soldiers went to war did not have a clue. The entire family went with them in ways most people could never understand.

Sitting at the table, Evan jealously watched several other couples laughing, touching, and sharing the moment and he thought of another reality for him that he had never gotten to explain to Rachel. He had given his heart fully to the belief that they had the rest of their lives together to share all the joys and the sadness that life possesses. She had given him her promise that she would always be there and that whenever she left, she would always return to him, not out of obligation, but because she wanted to. Evan had believed her with all of his being, so when she broke that promise, it tore a major hole in his ability to trust anyone. He now saw that even on incredibly important things like marriage, "forever" can really mean "for a little while," and he doubted he could ever put his heart on the line that fully again. There was too much potential to have it ripped out and shredded, and that hurt too much. Rachel had done that to him with such apparent ease and so casually that he knew there had been no point in trying to fight for what they had once had. She had made a military-like decision, cold and unfeeling, and nothing he could have said or done would have touched her heart at all. He had mentally put up his white flag and surrendered.

Evan had spent at least two years second-guessing himself about everything. What could he have changed? Could he have been more supportive somehow? Could he have been more romantic even though they were apart so much of the time? No matter how often he questioned himself, good answers always eluded him. There were so many priorities in Rachel's life that didn't include him that he couldn't logically find anything in his memory that could have changed their final results.

He had thought long and hard on the trust issue many times. She had never given him any reason to worry, but all their time apart had created some seeds of doubt for him anyway. She had been in several countries for extended periods of time in units consisting mostly of young men away from their homes too. He desperately wanted to believe she had been faithful to him, but after so much time and so much separation, he couldn't help but wonder. There was never any real reason to think the things he had begun to think, but he thought them anyway, and once that sled began moving down the hill, it was impossible to stop it. Every cold, brief e-mail; every story of a two-week mission in the countryside of Iraq; and a dozen other probably innocent things all helped trigger doubt in Evan's mind that Rachel was still his. He had hoped he was way off base and that he was not creating another self-fulfilling prophecy for himself, but he found himself always wondering just a little bit.

As he listened to the band begin its next song, he laughed to himself about how ridiculous and irrelevant those thoughts had been for him, and he was ashamed of how much time he had wasted thinking them. He knew that worry was such a waste of time and energy and rarely was productive for anyone, but none of that mattered now, and it was time to finally come back to life and join that party, and for the first time in a very long time, he felt ready to do that. The new possibilities excited him, and he couldn't stop his toes from tapping to the beat he heard.

There was a lively group of seven at the next table—three men and four women. Their toes were also tapping, and their shared laughter was contagious. They appeared to be slightly younger than Evan but not by much. He leaned over to the nearest male and started a conversation. "Hi. This band is really good, isn't it?"

The man turned and faced Evan. "Yes, they are. We're having a great time."

Evan smiled and replied, "As it should be." He raised his beer glass and toasted his new acquaintance.

"Are you here by yourself?" the man asked with some curiosity.

"Actually I am. I'm just here for a weekend away and thought this place looked fun."

"Well, come on over and join us. We've got plenty of room. I'm David."

"Thanks," stated Evan with a large smile. "I'd love to do that, and my name is Evan." With that, he left his table and slid into a chair at the table of his new friends.

Following some friendly introductions, he settled in and became a member of their party. The three couples were in Fort Myers on vacation, and the other woman was a local, who had been a lifelong friend of one of the wives. The group asked Evan a little about his background, and he was a bit reticent to fully open up right away.

"I'm just a Midwesterner who had some life cobwebs to clear out, and I thought a weekend here might help him do that." That answer seemed to suffice, and nobody pressed him further.

"We understand," several of them said at once. "You picked a good place to come to and relax."

"I think so," continued Evan. "So far the weekend has been mostly what I needed it to be, but I needed a night like this too. Thanks for letting me join in."

"Glad to hear that," said David cheerfully. "You're welcome here."

The sunburn on Evan's arms was already beginning to peel, and he could feel the heat from his chest and shoulders from under his shirt. It was a bit uncomfortable, but he didn't mind because he knew it was only temporary, and the warm sun had felt so good to him. He would be returning to snow and cold very soon, and after his weekend in the heat, the weather at home sounded quite unappealing. He reflected for a moment on the concept of temporary pain, and he thought of many areas in life where that ideal came into play. Doing without something in order to save money for something else seemed to qualify, though that pain wasn't a physical one. Exercising in order to lose weight was another temporary pain that came to his mind, and as he sat and thought, he came to realize, perhaps for the first time, the true measure of the pains people could really feel other than physical ones. Worrying about a spouse in the middle of a war was a type of pain he had undergone though none of it had been physical.

Evan had always tried to be cheerful and sought out humor in nearly everything he did. He had begun to notice the differences in himself for the past year, and it chilled him to think others had noticed them too. They must have though. When he did venture out of his house, which hadn't been all that often, he spent his time with intelligent, perceptive people, who noticed everything; and if they had seen his changes, he now silently thanked them for tolerating him anyway and for not holding his gloomy disposition against him.

His friends had always asked him about Rachel and how she was doing in Iraq.

Looking back, he knew now that his replies had gotten steadily shorter, and his smiles and enthusiasm had both lessened over time. He appreciated their concern for both Rachel and him, and he knew it was genuine, but a part of him had wished that there had been no such questions to answer. He wanted his wife to be with him so that there would have been no need for such questions, but she and the army had a different plan, and he had grown tired of explaining.

He had a magnetic bumper sticker that read, "Proud Husband of a Soldier." Rachel had bought it for him at the PX at the fort before she deployed. He happily displayed it on his car and panicked once when he lost it in the car wash. When he went back to retrieve it, the manager of the car wash had found it and returned it to him, and Evan had been quite relieved to get it back. There had been a time or two when he had tried to mentally create a bumper sticker that Rachel could display proudly on her vehicle that described him, but he had never come up with one.

The band was great, his new table partners were extremely friendly, and it was getting easier for Evan to find a smile. Two beers later, Evan found himself singing along with the band, laughing and carrying on like he used to several years earlier. He thought to himself that perhaps he really had succeeded this weekend. Maybe he had finally been able to let go. This group of welcoming strangers seemed to be the catalyst he had needed to allow himself to believe there was still fun in the world. It surprised him to realize just how unusual it felt to relax and have a good time with others. An odd feeling came over him as he thought of all the months he had wasted sitting alone. Life was meant to be lived no matter what, and from that weekend on, that was what he intended to do.

CHAPTER 19

The middle of March arrived, and the temperatures began to warm up. Winter was fighting to hang on, but spring showed its face with a lot more regularity than it had before. Every rain still brought extra hours for Evan in the basement, and he hated every minute he spent down there removing water. Another anniversary was just around the corner, but this time Evan was not the least bit excited about it. Days that had once been so special to him had evolved into painful reminders that he was living a married life alone. He went shopping and filled a box with snacks and paperbacks and some other things he knew Rachel enjoyed but didn't have at the Baghdad PX. He searched for a short while in the card section at Walmart and found a semi-romantic anniversary card to place in the box before he mailed it. This time the process seemed to him more like an obligatory routine than an act of genuine passion. It had generally taken a week for Rachel to receive the things he had previously sent her, so he made sure he mailed the box in plenty of time to reach her by their anniversary date.

The days ticked by like molasses, and when their actual anniversary date arrived, Evan spent most of the day moping around the house. He could not force himself to be cheerful in any way and had no real desire to leave the house or be around others. He checked his e-mail every hour or so but found nothing there except spam, and the only thing in the outside mailbox was a water bill. All the thoughts and doubts he had about himself and his marriage floated to the surface of his mind, and he did little to sink them. He later came to understand that when a person is depressed, negative thoughts can appear to be a welcome friend at times, though he didn't realize that on that day.

By late afternoon, he had given up hope of hearing anything from his wife. It was after midnight in Baghdad, and he doubted that an e-mail would appear that late.

Outside, the sky was turning grayer by the minute, and it seemed to be a nice match to Evan's mood inside the house. He had grown sadly used to seeing special days come and go without any type of celebration, and he believed that distance certainly played a part in everything, but with modern technology, distance and the military didn't account for everything.

Evan knew how detailed Rachel was with her schedule, and events such as birthdays and anniversaries did not sneak up on anyone, especially her. He was extremely despondent to think of the huge gap that existed between how he had originally pictured spending romantic anniversaries and his reality of spending each of their first three anniversary dates entirely by himself.

He tried to imagine himself being distracted or busy enough to ever forget either Rachel's birthday or their anniversary, and he knew that he would never do that. He liked the extra fun of those special days, the planning of something new to make the occasion memorable, and he wished that Rachel did those things the same way he did. Any sign of warmth or caring from her would have been a welcome treasure for him, but those signs were absent. As the afternoon turned into another quiet, lonely night, Evan cooked a hamburger for himself and tried really hard not to continually feel empty. He thought about going to bed early but had no desire to do that because he knew all he would do there was lie awake and think even more, so he looked for another type of mental diversion.

It seemed the more he tried to think of cheerful things, the less he was able to succeed. He looked at Rachel's picture on top of the television and tried to smile. At the moment, he couldn't really see a future, so he allowed his thoughts to be swallowed up by the past. For a few moments, it was as if the Rachel in the picture, the one from three years earlier, was there in the room with him, and he thought back to laughs and smiles and trips together. He thought of holding hands while walking on a beach and sharing time at an airport during an adventure to a new place. He remembered the childlike wonder of Rachel as she experienced Las Vegas for the first time as an adult, and he relived the joy of sharing her first round of golf.

There had been so many wonderful moments while they dated. They hated it when they were apart and couldn't wait to be together again. How could anyone have dreamed up the mountains that had appeared in the road of their relationship? The worst thought Evan had was when he realized that even if he had climbed those mountains and gotten to the other side, it would not have mattered.

It was as though the television stars were all aligned against Evan that night. After he finished his anniversary hamburger, he relaxed in his recliner and hunted for a show to watch. The first station had *Saving Private Ryan*, and though he really liked that movie, he wasn't in the mood for anything remotely close to a military story. The next channel was showing *Sahara*, which was a little too visually close to the Iraq desert for his liking. The next two channels were sitcoms he didn't really care for, so he kept surfing. *You've Got Mail* caused Evan to sigh aloud because it instantly reminded him that he didn't have mail on that day. Three channels further down the dial, he came to a Rambo movie, and Rambo would not work on that night either. He could feel the weight of his karma, and he gave up on the television and turned on his Nintendo game system to escape with some mindless play time.

He remained subdued the remainder of the night, sad about being alone, sad that the army had become an opponent he had to face, and sad that he had not heard from his wife on yet another anniversary apart. Sleep did not come easily for Evan that night, and just like being alone during the day, he was getting very used to not sleeping well in his bed alone each night.

Three days after their anniversary, Evan got the e-mail he had been looking for. It was one paragraph long and told of how busy she had been.

Hey, Sorry I didn't get this to you sooner, but I've been swamped. They are keeping me hopping here with twelve- to-fourteen-hour shifts. More guard duty at the palace too and lots of gym time when I'm not working. Other than that, not much else. Hope you are okay.

Me

Evan stared at the computer screen and didn't know quite what to feel. There was nothing warm in the message at all, and there was no mention of the box or the card he had sent her. He had no idea how or when to reply to her. She hadn't even mentioned their anniversary.

April came and went without any major events except the arrival of spring. Evan mowed the yard nearly every week and made sure the bills were paid. The days got warmer, but the nights were still long. Near the end of the month, another thought hit him hard, and he actually found himself feeling nervous. Rachel's tour was coming to an end. Her unit was scheduled to return home before the end of May. Every other time Rachel had been gone, he couldn't wait for her to return to him, but his time it felt different. He knew he had changed, and he felt equally confident that Rachel had also changed. He had no real idea what effect a year in a war zone could have on a person, but he knew it would be naïve to believe the girl he had dated and married was the same one who forgot anniversaries and sent cold, unfeeling e-mails to him.

She would be back in a few short weeks. He felt ashamed at how uncomfortable that fact made him. Would they have anything to talk about? Would any of their predeployment romantic fire still burn? Would all their time apart take its toll on both of them and lead them in separate directions? Every bit of worry and anxiety Evan had felt for the past year suddenly magnified tenfold, and he could not find even a moment of peace and comfort.

Prior to meeting Rachel, the only time Evan had ever thought about the military was when he saw a story on the news or read one in the paper. Once she entered his world, all that changed, and when she was deployed, it all changed again. The nightly news had become part of his routine, and he had become a regular MSNBC viewer. Politics and war were now more real to Evan than he could have ever imagined, and he remembered several times when he had e-mailed news to Rachel that directly affected her, and prior to Evan telling her about those things, she knew nothing of them. Those moments mystified him and made him wonder how much the military leaders actually told their soldiers. Evan found it incredible that there were multiple times when the rest of the world knew more about her immediate situation than she did. He was now a news guy, a seeker of daily knowledge and information regarding the war in Iraq and the policy makers in Washington, who made the decisions that directly affected his wife, his life, and his marriage.

He was relatively sure that Rachel was as safe as a soldier could be in Baghdad, but every report of a roadside bomb or a missile attack still made the hair on his neck stand up. War had never been real to him before, and he didn't like its realities now, but he knew that for him, war could never again just be an abstract concept that only involved others. For him, that line had been forever crossed, and he could not ever again pretend to be naïve to all its ramifications.

Rarely an hour went by when he didn't think about Rachel's tour ending and having her home once again. She had already indicated that she had no desire to return to teaching, and that added to the nervous edge Evan constantly felt. She was now a soldier with a desire to become a full-time soldier, and he had no clue where that would lead her, him, or them.

Evan didn't like how fast he had seemingly become an outsider in his wife's army world, and no matter what future pictures he created in his mind, no matter what job or career he would eventually have, he could not see how he could ever fully enter her military life. His not working a regular job while she was gone had seemed to increase the speed with which the two appeared to grow apart. The distance between Baghdad and home was just a formality, and Evan feared the two could now be seven thousand miles apart in the same room.

The anxiety kept building for Evan as the calendar changed from April to May, very quickly counting down the days to Rachel's return. Rachel's mom was the antithesis of Evan. Whenever he talked with her or saw her, she bubbled with excitement and energy at the thought of her daughter's safe return home. Evan wished with all his heart that he could share her excitement, but he couldn't.

During the first week in May, a totally unexpected thing happened, and when Evan looked back on it, he knew without a doubt that that event totally changed the path of the rest of his life. It began as just another morning. Evan grabbed some coffee and watched a few minutes of the morning news, but when they began repeating their stories, he turned off the television and strolled to his computer to check his e-mail. The normal quota of daily spam messages were there waiting to be deleted, but there was also a message from Rachel. He thought it was probably an update on the details of her return to the States, but what he read totally caught him off guard.

Like her other spring e-mails, there was very little fluff in it. She got directly to the point, as if casual conversation with Evan had become a chore. She laid her idea out in a matter-of-fact way, suggesting to him that what he was about to read had already been decided. When his initial shock wore off, Evan could feel the nerves and worries that had been plaguing him begin to disappear. He read the e-mail again to make sure his eyes had not deceived him.

Hi, Hope everything is good at home. I've been talking with a colonel here, who is impressed with my work, and he told me he'd love to have me, or a worker like me, for another year. I've honestly enjoyed my year here, and staying another year makes sense to me for lots of reasons, so I'm gonna stay.

Evan knew that Rachel relished the praise of a superior just like most people do. Service in a war zone accelerated her military retirement income and gave her a greater chance of being noticed by other superior officers. Those kinds of contacts could be extremely helpful to her career and her future, and she had talked before about liking the thought of another year of tax-free income. The e-mail continued.

The paperwork for all this has been in the works for about a month, so when my unit comes home in a couple weeks, I'll be staying. I'll go see them off, but after that I'll start my new duties. My mailing address will change, and I'll e-mail that to you when I get it.

Me

Evan studied the message carefully. She had mapped out another year in her life, in their lives, without even a hint of discussion with him. It was all about her and her thoughts and wishes. He was again amazed at how eager she was to spend another year in Iraq. His first thought was that the news stories he had been seeing must have been greatly exaggerated. Bombs appeared to still be going off there, missiles seemed to still be flying, and people were still dying there daily; yet his wife had volunteered to spend more time right in the middle of it and away from him and the safety of home.

Evan and Rachel had been married for thirty-seven months, and because of the army and Rachel's unquenchable thirst to see the world, they had been apart for twenty-six of those months, and now they faced the prospect of another year in different countries. The anxiety Evan had felt about Rachel's return now switched to a fear of the next year that lay ahead. At some point, the realities of being together again would happen, and Evan wondered if it would be better or worse to prolong that for twelve more months. He hated being alone at home without her, and now he could see that there was a lot more solitary time in his future. He saw visions of the many dreams he and Rachel had once shared shattering into small pieces, and there was nothing he could see that would glue them together. He got sadder by the minute that morning and had no real idea what to think or do next.

Another year without a job did not excite him either, but the prospects of getting one were slim. The US economy had faltered unexpectedly, and unemployment numbers were rising faster than a flooded river. He had already tried several times to find various types of work to complement the networking business, but the only real offers he had received were from insurance companies that were willing to hire anyone, and that didn't interest him at all. Time after time, he was reminded of how unqualified, at least on paper, a teacher was for anything else besides teaching.

He had given his resume and credentials to at least a dozen companies in four different states but had not heard back from any of them. The jobs he had applied for ranged from a parking valet to maintenance at a fancy country club, but day after day, he continued to sit at home alone, sometimes wishing for his old job back and, other times, not caring at all how his days were being spent. He knew that whether he had a job or not, his nights would still be spent alone, and he was losing interest in everything.

Evan could foresee part of the year ahead and knew that as cold as some of Rachel's e-mails had been recently, they might get even colder in the future. He could also foresee that before long, the main topic of their e-mails would be money and bills, and he didn't see anything pleasant about that. He had saved up enough to take care of things at home for over a year, but without a regular income, that money would run out long before her second tour ended.

He could already hear her thoughts, and he couldn't really blame her for thinking them. She would feel that he wasn't doing his part while she was doing more than her share in Iraq. Her main goal, besides the military goals, was to get ahead with some loans she had at home, and he could now envision her believing she was just spinning her wheels financially and not making any gains. His job hunting would continue, but he wasn't optimistic about finding one that would actually help enough to make a difference. He mused to himself about how much money he had accumulated back when he was single, and more than once, he would have liked to have gone back to that level of freedom and independence; but he knew that was not possible at that moment in his life.

Evan could see his and Rachel's roles reversing from the typical couple. Evan was no longer a provider, and his self-esteem was dropping as quickly as his bank account total was. He had been steadily withdrawing from the world while Rachel's wings had begun to fully spread. Every time Evan felt angry and frustrated with the army and how it had changed his life, he wanted to do something drastic like selling his house and just leaving for somewhere new, but most of the time, the guilt of doing something like that to a deployed soldier kept him in check. When Rachel forgot his birthdays or their anniversaries and his frustration boiled over, he thought of a lot of things he was not proud of. Each day he spent alone made him long for human closeness, wherever he might find it, and every day he felt stuck at home made him wish to be anywhere else. He even spent one full month drinking a lot to try and escape the person he had become and the life he was living, but that didn't work and it got very expensive.

Life for Evan had become an equation that would never balance. As Rachel got stronger and more independent in her uniform, Evan became weaker and less secure with himself. Now whenever someone asked him about Rachel, he secretly cringed before he answered. He told people what he knew they wanted to hear but rarely elaborated and tried to change the subject quickly if he could. Sometimes he avoided situations where he knew he would be with others who would inquire about Rachel just so he wouldn't hear the questions. Usually it was his networking friends who asked him the most questions, but if he went to a high school ball game, other teachers they had both worked with quizzed him as well.

Evan couldn't count all the thoughts that raced around in his mind after reading Rachel's e-mail. As he sat and gazed at the words on the computer screen, he tried to formulate the reply he would send her. He had no idea what he would write and decided to think about it a while rather than just typing an impulsive, poorly worded response to her bombshell. He made himself believe that a few hours of thought would help to put the right words in his mouth so that he could answer in a tactful, honest manner. Part of him didn't think that any amount of time and care would matter since he remembered that the issue had already been settled, and Rachel had decided everything. His input was mostly irrelevant because nothing he could say would change her mind or change her decision, but still, he wanted to answer her carefully and with some thought.

CHAPTER 20

E van spent the rest of the night thinking of an appropriate response to Rachel's e-mail. He so badly wanted to get the words right that he wrote down a draft on paper. Then he edited it, reedited it, and changed things at least four more times before he was satisfied. He wanted to strike the best balance possible between showing his support and conveying his concerns. The following morning, when he believed he was ready, he sat at his computer and typed the reply to Rachel.

Wow, that's some major news! I was getting ready to welcome you home, and now that will have to wait for a whole year. When I read your message, I thought of Ernest Hemingway and how he eagerly signed up to be in a war. I'm not sure I'll ever fully understand the enthusiasm you show for being there, but I'm trying. I'm sure you're great at what you do, and I know staying will help your career, but you'll have to excuse me for not being totally excited about your second tour. From this end, all I see is the danger surrounding you and another year here by myself. You can get me your new address when you know it. I trust that you've thought all this out and you know what you're doing. I'll do my best to keep things going here, and I'll hope every day that all of this is a good thing for both of us. Right now, I'm having a hard time thinking it is.

Me

He reread his reply and made sure everything was typed correctly, and then he clicked send. After that, he just sat and gazed blankly. It dawned on him again that another year of his life was about to be shaped and directed and dictated by outside forces. He had always been in control before, and now it seemed that everything in his life was out of his control, and it all happened without his input or consent, and it made him queasy.

The army had turned into an opponent that he could not defeat. He had been truthful in his e-mail when he wrote that he would never be able to fully understand or appreciate its allure, but he really had tried. The bonding and sense of belonging and importance must surely be at a level he could never grasp, and he had seen countless evidence from Rachel that proved to him that any time there was a choice for her between her uniform and her husband, he would always finish in second place.

After he sent his e-mail to Rachel, he was in no real mood to do anything productive. He went to the living room and finished his coffee and considered the next few hours as well as the next year. Just before noon, he called Jordan to see what he was doing.

"Nothing much," stated Jordan. "Just working in the shop. Come on over if you want."

"I'll be over shortly."

Evan parked his car outside Jordan's shop building and walked slowly toward the door. He could hear the air wrench either loosening or tightening some bolts, and he smiled a little at Jordan's love of big machinery. He opened the door, and the noise got much louder. When Jordan saw Evan, he looked up for a moment and then finished the work he was doing with the air wrench.

"Hey," hollered Jordan over the noise of the wrench.

"Hey yourself," answered Evan even though he didn't think Jordan could hear his words. The two spoke so often that catching up on things generally didn't take long. Evan must have worn his mood on his face because when Jordan looked up again, he immediately put down his wrench and stopped working. They both flipped over buckets and sat down, and then the real conversation began.

"What's wrong?" asked Jordan.

"Got a little news that kind of kicked my butt," responded Evan.

"What's that? Must be something good."

"Oh, it is," continued Evan. "Not only is Rachel not going to be home in a couple weeks, she's staying over there for another year." Evan let that sentence sink in for a second, and then he repeated it. "She's staying for another year."

"Damn, what brought that on?" inquired Jordan. "Did you piss her off?"

Evan laughed at that comment, but it helped lighten the mood. "Maybe so. Hadn't thought of it quite that way, but I guess it's possible."

Jordan then asked the magic question. "So what do you think about that?" It was at that moment that Evan realized something for the first time, and he felt instantly weak, and that must have shown on his face too because Jordan hesitated with his follow-up question. "Are you okay?"

"I'm okay," stated Evan. "It just dawned on me that through all this, she has never asked me what you just did, about what I think about it all. She had been putting this second year together for over a month." He shook his head in helplessness as he spoke. "For a whole month she has known that she was staying for another year and never told me any of it, never even a hint. This is just another house in Panama and a resort in Guatemala except this time the plan is actually going to happen. She always seems to have a plan cooking in her mind, and I never seem to be anywhere in the decision-making process anymore. Maybe she should know that she pisses me off too!"

They both laughed at that comment, but Evan had meant it. "I wish I knew just how much the military has changed the way she thinks about things. I obviously have no clue anymore. When we first started dating and getting serious, we talked about everything before we did anything, especially the big things that affected us both. I guess I've changed a lot in how I think too. I don't really know anymore."

"You're the same guy to me," interjected Jordan. "A little gloomier than usual today, but other than that, nothing is different."

"I just feel stuck. I'm here in a routine that we used to share, and now it's all mine, and she has a new one. I'm always at home, and she has found the whole world. It would be silly of me to not think she has changed, but I can't believe she is totally a different person. I hope not anyway. It just makes me mad that I don't seem to be in any part of her plans anymore. I don't know anything until it has already been decided by her or others."

"I know. That has to be tough."

Evan and Jordan sat and talked for another hour or so, and Evan appreciated having his friend's ear to bend. "I hate seeing you like this. Part of why I like hanging with you is your humor and your energy, and now you're quiet all the time, and your energy level looks pretty low to me. We need to fix that no matter what else is going on. You still have to live."

"I know. I'll work on that. I promise," said Evan with a subtle smile.

On his way home, Evan drove by the golf course. The parking lot was crowded, and he recognized many of his friends' cars. It was a beautiful spring day, and he was momentarily tempted to pull in and lose himself for several hours. He drove on, however, and soon was back home. When he got inside, he again felt the emptiness of his house, which had become his norm. The reality of Rachel's second tour was still fresh and sinking in fully. It had taken a couple weeks to mentally prepare for her return, and now he had to come to grips with being alone for another year. He began thinking of all the newscasts he would still be compelled to watch. No matter how safe Rachel told him she was, every report of troop surges and attacks still got his full attention. He could never totally rid himself of the thought that at any minute of any day, she could be killed. It irritated him whenever she talked casually about being there because no matter what she said, he knew that danger was always very close. She was in the middle of a war zone.

He even felt guilty at times for some of the things he thought.

During more than one of his restless nights, he had lain in bed and pondered the worst. He feared a phone call from the Department of Defense informing him of some tragic accident. He could hear some sympathetic voice on the line, telling him how proud he should be of Rachel and her service. He had even allowed himself to think about the huge life insurance policy she had taken out on herself. He had laughed at the irony of thinking of putting a price on a person's life. He knew life insurance was necessary and was a good thing in general, but he never felt good when he thought about having that really large check. No matter how distant he and Rachel had seemed to grow, he could never justify trading her life for money. It always felt odd to imagine that most unwelcome phone call, but for the past year, he knew it could come at any time. Now he had to deal with all that for yet another year.

He wondered if Rachel ever had thoughts like those while she sat or worked or patrolled in the desert of Iraq. What things filled her mind during her downtime? Evan had come to realize that since she had begun travelling the world with the army, he really had no idea what she thought about or dreamed about on a daily basis. He used to know because she told him, and they had talked about those kinds of things, but now they were never in the same place, so their conversations no longer strayed to dreams or what-ifs. Their e-mails now were all about the necessities, not the extras, and the rare phone calls had minute limitations on them, so there was no time to be wasted on frivolous hypotheticals. Monthly bills and payments were generally the topic of discussion though occasionally some other news worked its way into an e-mail or a conversation.

Evan sat around the house most of the rest of the day. He grabbed his pitching wedge and chipped golf balls in the backyard a couple different times, but most of the time he spent pretending to watch TV and trying to imagine Rachel's response to his e-mail reply. He had tried to be honest and supportive and wondered if he had accomplished his goal. Had she read it and smiled? Or maybe frowned? Did his reply even matter to her? Did she expect him to be excited about her second tour? She had lined everything up without his knowledge or approval, so Evan finally decided that his excitement or lack of excitement was probably irrelevant to her.

He tried his best to imagine the year that lay ahead for him. He knew he needed to find another job, but those prospects still looked rather dim. The economy was still in turmoil, and hundreds of thousands of people were losing their jobs every month, so very few places were looking to actually hire anyone. Each time he applied for a position and either heard nothing from them or received a letter of rejection, his self-confidence sank even further. For many reasons, he knew the upcoming year would not be an enjoyable one for him.

The third week in May, Evan got another interesting e-mail from Rachel. Her original unit was heading home from Iraq, and she was apparently feeling a little strange about waving good-bye to them and remaining behind.

> *Hi, I'm getting ready to start the new job and am looking forward to it. My other unit is heading home tomorrow, so we're celebrating tonight. It's odd to be thinking that they'll be gone and I'll be staying. Several of them told me they think I'm nuts for staying. They can't wait to get home to their lives and families. Lots of hugs and stories taking place here, but it's all good. Hope everything there is good too.*
>
> *Me*

It was interesting to Evan to read some actual emotion from one of Rachel's e-mails. She had not shown any of that to him in quite a while. After he realized her emotions all stemmed from her bonds with her fellow soldiers and not because she missed being at home, he closed the e-mail and thought no more about it.

June arrived and brought with it steady rains. Evan once again found himself a prisoner to his basement and his wet vac. Hour after hour, day after day, for ten straight days, he did little but remove water. After the previous flooding, he had given up on putting their nice things back down there, so there was now nothing down there to ruin. In fact, he had bought several large plastic tubes and had begun packing away Rachel's clothes and other things he knew he wouldn't need or use in the upcoming year.

The idea had come to him shortly after he became aware of her second tour. Part of it seemed practical and logical to him, and part of it seemed like a head start on the inevitable. The practical view he took was that if he applied for and got a job in another state then he would have to move. Moving required packing, and since Rachel's things would not be used anyway, he thought it could be a good idea to have them all boxed up and in one place. Once he began the process, he was amazed at how many clothes she had. It struck him as ironic that someone who now wore only an army uniform every day had so many outfits that he thought might never again be worn by her.

The pessimistic side of his packing troubled him a bit, but he followed through and finished anyway. He thought that if he and Rachel continued to grow apart as they had been doing, there was a chance they could go their separate ways when she returned, and having all her things already sorted would make that unhappy time go a little more easily. If she got home and wanted their marriage to really work, unpacking her things would be a very simple thing to do. As Evan stacked the last tub of Rachel's things, he paused to consider which of the two ways it would really go.

CHAPTER 21

The future was something Evan had always planned for and looked forward to. There were always new goals to work toward and new projects to complete, so living without a purpose had never been a factor for him. He had often watched others existing rather than living, and although he could never truly identify with them, he felt sorry for them and their lack of direction. Now, sadly, he had begun to not only understand those people, but he could identify with them because he recognized that he had become one of them. He felt like an armless man, who had been placed in the middle of a lake in a canoe. He had no real control of his vessel and was at the mercy of whatever direction the wind and waves carried him, and he could not know which side of the shore he would eventually reach or how long it would take to reach it. As the heat of summer bore down on him, he could not remember the last time he had felt good about himself. Every time he walked into his house, the outside heat disappeared, and all he could feel was the cold of being alone.

He ached to return to his cheerful, optimistic, energetic self, but he could no longer find that person inside himself. When he stood before the morning mirror, all he saw was a hollow shell of the man he used to be and longed to be again. It pained him more than he cared to admit that being apart from Rachel had dramatically weakened him while her absence from him had seemed to make her grow stronger. He had always believed their mutual strength had come from each other and from being together. He knew she had leaned on him for support and encouragement prior to deploying, but that didn't happen anymore. Had everything really changed that much? He still wanted and needed her, but he wondered every day if she still needed or wanted him. He knew that time would answer all his questions, but he also knew the time would be agonizing and lonely until those answers appeared. Eventually the two would again be face to face, alone and close, and he didn't see any way that moment could be comfortable or easy.

Being a part of her military world had always been difficult, and now it seemed impossible. He had been interested in her drill weekends and PT tests and the trainings and schools she had attended, and although he knew he never got the entire story of the things she did on base, he had simply learned to live with that. He had eaten as much of that pie as she had put on the table, but now it seemed to him that he was outside the deli being forced to settle with occasionally just looking through the window at all the pies.

The third weekend in June, Evan's networking company held a national convention in Orlando, and he began to prepare for the trip. He knew he really didn't have enough money to go, but he had paid in advance and did not want to waste the money he had already spent. He and Jordan had already purchased their plane tickets and had an expensive hotel room booked for four nights. Two other team members would also share their room to help keep costs down as much as possible, and the four would meet up once everyone arrived in Florida.

Evan really enjoyed his company's conventions. He got to see friends from all over the country, and he never failed to get inspired from the words he heard from the speakers on stage. His only real issue on this trip was his limited cash supply, but he knew he would find a way to make it work. He debated with himself several times whether or not to even tell Rachel he was going, and he finally decided not to tell her. It wouldn't matter one way or another to her, and if it did matter, he concluded that he did not want to hear a long-distance lecture on excessive spending. It only took him an hour to get everything organized and packed, and the only thing left was to pick up Jordan and head to the airport. He had to laugh at how much easier it was to find his suits and other clothes in the closet now that Rachel's things were all packed away.

Evan drove to Jordan's house, and he was ready and waiting. Jordan didn't get many opportunities to get away from home and was extremely excited to be heading to Orlando. He didn't much like flying though, and his apprehension showed more than he probably wished it did. As they both fastened their seatbelts in the plane Evan, tried his best to tell some jokes and lighten the mood for his friend.

"I can't get this damn buckle fastened. I sure hope the rest of the plane isn't broken like this thing is," said Evan as he pretended it was faulty. He pulled and twisted it until Jordan offered to help. Then Evan started laughing and Jordan understood.

"Not funny, buddy," Jordan replied seriously.

Did you see that little crack in the wing when we walked in? Hope it's okay," continued Evan.

"Good grief, that's enough already!" barked Jordan. "You're a goofball."

"Hey, I got you to at least smile a little. Just take it easy. The flight will be great, and we'll be there before you know it."

Evan's attempt at humor seemed to work, because when the plane was high in the sky and at its cruising altitude, Jordan relaxed and began to enjoy the start of his vacation.

Once on the ground in Orlando, the pair hailed a cab and took in all the sites they could see under the Florida twilight sky as they rode to the convention hotel. The Ramada that hosted the convention was like a small town all to itself and was quite impressive. Someone had told Evan that it was the largest Ramada in the world, and as the cab approached the complex, Evan had no trouble believing that fact was true.

They checked in, and with more than a little effort, they eventually found the correct hallway that led to their room. Once the slacks and dress shirts were unfolded and hung up, they stepped out onto their private deck. The view from the fifteenth floor was amazing. Directly below them lay the hotel's private golf course, perfectly manicured and immediately a temptation to Evan. Farther out on the horizon, they could make out what appeared to be the top of the castle from Disney World. Evan and Jordan smiled at each other, partly because of the beauty they were seeing and partly because the realization that they were away from home for a few days had finally sunk in. "Pretty nice, isn't it?" began Evan.

"We're definitely not at home anymore," Jordan laughed. "Let's go get some food."

They were both hungry, so they went back downstairs to find something to eat. It took less than thirty seconds of walking in the hallway before they ran into people Evan knew. They were three team members from Colorado, who had just finished their dinner, and they recommended one of the bar and grills inside the hotel. Evan and Jordan took their advice and made their way there.

Before their food arrived, several other team members had found their way into the same bar. It was impossible to count the handshakes or measure the width of the smiles as friendships once again were rekindled. Immediately, Evan knew he had made the right decision in coming to the convention, and as he and Jordan ate their meals, their table filled up with people and a night of drinking, storytelling, and laughter got fully underway.

It only took an hour before someone asked Evan about Rachel. He knew it was inevitable, but he had hoped to put the questioning off longer than one short hour. He put on his usual smile and answered the best he could. "As far as I know, she's fine," he told the questioner. "She's just beginning a second tour." Nobody else except Jordan knew that she had chosen to stay another year, so he had already prepared his answer and his explanation when his friends inquired about her. "She had a great chance to advance her military career, and she took it, so she'll be there another year or so." He was certain that many more would ask, and he was more right than even he had imagined. For the next three days and nights, Evan was bombarded by more than two dozen friends, who were concerned for both Rachel and him. He got several hugs and pats on the back as people tried their best to empathize with what he was going through. They all were sincere and meant well, so Evan did his best to smile and reassure them that both he and Rachel would be all right. He wished that his private thoughts were equally optimistic.

One of the most emotionally difficult moments of the trip for Evan came the first day of the event during the opening ceremonies, when the company gave their salute to all the veterans. It was an impressive presentation on the giant screens, filled with scores of patriotic images all moving to the backdrop of "God Bless the USA." He knew before he arrived that the veterans' salute would be part of the program, and he could never predict how he would react to it. Eight months earlier at the regional rally in Des Moines, those putting on the event had done a similar veterans' salute, but they had used Toby Keith's "American Soldier" as the music that accompanied the slideshow. Evan remembered how he had suddenly and surprisingly found tears streaming down both his cheeks. The pictures on the screen then were of Arlington Cemetery and showed family members weeping and hugging, and it had all become far too real for Evan.

He remembered trying in vain to hide his obviously visible emotions from the others near him, but he quickly gave up on that idea. Emotions and honest feelings were a large part of his network company's strength, and everyone around him knew his situation. He was worried about his wife dying in a war in a foreign land, and it was as simple as that. When the song finished, he had dried his eyes and cheeks as best he could and attempted to refocus his thoughts back on the positive excitement of the day.

In Orlando, as the presentation dominated the huge hall, Evan stood motionless and attentive, but his emotions were not stirred like they had been in Des Moines. He wondered to himself what the difference was, but he knew the answer. Eight more months alone had taken its toll on how near the surface he allowed his emotions to get. He had gotten really good at keeping his feelings buried deep, and the presentation he had been watching was not enough to bring them out. In his youth, Evan had been a master at hiding his emotions, but as he matured, he had learned to show them and share them more. Now it seemed that in some respects, he had come full circle, and he was secretly not proud of that.

He had come across so many unfeeling people in his life, and he had never wanted to be like them. He believed that emotions were evidence that a person was alive, and it bothered him to think that a wonderful part of who he was had died, or at least was dying. He vowed to himself that he would once again find his emotions and would feel and care about life like he had used to.

The second night of the convention, his group's leaders hosted a team meeting in one of the hotel ballrooms. With five thousand people at the convention, it was easy to miss seeing someone, and the team meeting was a great chance to make sure all the team members got together in one place to celebrate successes and bond even further. Things were generally kept quite informal at the team meetings, and this one began that way too. Then something quite unexpected happened. The group's leader, Chris, a close friend of Evan's, changed the tone of the meeting for a moment and began talking about Rachel and her service. He talked with pride to the entire group about having a teammate who was willing to go to war to protect us at home, and he spoke with genuine emotion because he had served in Vietnam, and he knew firsthand what being in a war zone and being away from loved ones meant.

Evan felt a lump grow in his throat as Chris continued. "Evan, would you please stand up? For those who don't know, Evan's wife, Rachel, has been serving in Iraq for a year, and we just found out that she will be staying for a second tour. I'd like to take just a minute to recognize both of them for her service and his sacrifices at home and ask that each of you keep both of them in your prayers."

Evan stood as requested and then felt a bit embarrassed when the entire room broke into a long round of applause. He didn't know what to do or say, and he felt that he had done nothing that deserved applause, but after half a minute, he simply waved and quietly uttered, "Thank you, everyone," and then he sat back down. "I'll pass on all your good wishes to Rachel."

When the team meeting concluded, Evan was amazed at how many people sought him out to offer their concerns and prayers. Most asked him to thank Rachel for them, and he, of course, said he would. That night reinforced to him what he had already come to know. The people in this company were incredibly giving and kind, and he always felt better when he was with them. He had not known Chris was going to do what he did, but he left the meeting truly touched and moved by the love he had been shown. His only sad thought was that even when he told Rachel about all that had happened, she would never be able to fully appreciate it and what it had meant to him. When he was finally able to leave the meeting, he wished that Rachel could have been there so all these great friends could have thanked her in person and not with a message sent through him. Things were always lost in translation, and he doubted he could convey the true power of what the night had made him feel. He would try his best though because most of the prayers were for her, even though many of them had never met her.

The last two days of the convention were filled with fun and learning, capped off with a gala banquet on Saturday night. The questions about Rachel diminished, and Evan credited that to the idea that most of the people who knew them both or knew just him had already asked about her. The band at the gala was outstanding, and they had the room jumping and cheering and dancing as they turned out their versions of some of rock and roll's classic songs. Evan hated to see midnight arrive because that meant the gala was coming to an end. Jordan found Evan when the music stopped, and they went back to the table, where they had sat for the meal.

Several friends were at the table, and none of them was in a hurry to bring the night to a conclusion. Evan and Jordan's plane left at 6:00 AM, and someone suggested they go to Evan's room and talk and drink some more. Sleep seemed pointless and unnecessary since they would have to be up and gone in just four short hours to make sure they had time to get through airport security.

There were eight people in Evan and Jordan's room, and the evening's fun definitely continued. Laughter and stories were intertwined with some serious moments as everyone reflected on the convention. Goals were set, and accountability partners were established, and everyone verbally recommitted himself to raising the level of his business. Each secretly hoped he would follow through once he got home.

Evan and Jordan packed all their things while the group talked around them, and before anyone knew it 4:00 AM arrived, and it was time to leave for the airport. Good-byes were said, and hugs were shared. Evan stood with Jordan on the deck one last time in an attempt to admire the view and to embed it in their memories. Even at this early hour, he could see lights and activity in every direction, another reminder that he was not at home. "I guess it's time to go," stated Jordan with a hint of regret in his voice. "Yeah, it is," replied Evan. "Time to get back to the real world."

Evan slept nearly the entire flight home and smiled just a little when the plane landed, and he knew the trip was over. Now it was back to reality, and he hoped he could build on the feelings he had experienced in Orlando. He knew that he had to, no matter what, or else he would become someone that not even he would be able to recognize or want to spend time with. The weekend had been a full one and had reawakened him to many things he hadn't wanted to think about for quite a while, and now it was up to him to bring those things to life.

He dropped Jordan off at his house to the smiles and the hugs of his children, who had obviously missed him, and then he drove home. Once in his house again, he thought about the necessary changes in his level of discipline required to reach the goals he had set that weekend, and he was determined to do that. He walked back to his computer and sat down. He had an e-mail to write to Rachel that would try and convey all the support she had from their friends. He sighed and began to type.

CHAPTER 22

Evan still looked for jobs at least a couple times a week but received no offers. His networking business had become stagnant over the past year for several reasons, but the primary one was because of Evan's lack of work and his lack of commitment to consistent activity. He knew that for his business to surge like he wanted it to, he would have to work a lot smarter than he had been doing.

He had come to realize there was a huge gap between being busy and being productive, and he had gotten extremely good at creating the illusion of being busy. A networking business is all about sharing with others and combining that with devouring all the personal growth material possible. Evan had been reading the books and listening to the CDs, but he had spent the lion's share of his time alone at home, so the sharing part of the business had been severely neglected.

It would have been incredibly easy for Evan to fall back into the same rut he had been living in prior to the Orlando trip, and he knew it. He was still alone and would be by himself for many more months. If he enjoyed any successes, Rachel would not be there to share them with him, so his motivation level was still fairly low. Throughout July, Evan made a concerted effort to leave the house more often than usual. He had always attended every luncheon and rally that his company held in the area, but now he went to local restaurants more often for lunch, attended ball games at his former high school, and just became generally more visible around town.

One drawback to seeing more people in town was that he got more questions about Rachel. He still watched the news every day in order to know what was happening in Iraq because he still wanted to remain informed. He secretly always searched for a glimpse of Rachel every time he saw a reporter do a story from Baghdad, but he never saw her. Apparently his friends and other townspeople were doing the same thing because several people made comments to him about watching for her on television. The level of people's concern for both Rachel and him never ceased to amaze and impress him.

When people asked about Rachel, all he could do was give them the same answer he had always given. "As far as I know, she's fine." He didn't know much more than that himself, so he could never be more specific than that. He was happy that, in most cases, his simple answer seemed to be enough for whoever asked him about her.

The summer ended up as long and unproductive for Evan as the previous winter had been. No matter what he tried to do to motivate himself, he found it exceedingly difficult to sustain his efforts for longer than a few days at a time. He had gotten interested in the upcoming presidential election and the coverage of the rallies, and the speeches grabbed his attention for hours at a time.

Phone calls from Rachel had gotten quite rare over the summer, but there were e-mails at least a couple times a week. He still checked e-mails every day just in case, but he had come to understand that even if something major happened to her, she would not write the whole truth to him. Part of her had to know that he worried about her a lot, and she went out of her way to convey her safety, or at least the perception of safety, to him. After everything he saw on the news, he knew he could never be convinced of anyone's complete safety in Iraq at this time in history. Danger was always just around the corner for everyone there.

This tour was very different than the first one for Rachel. For her first year in Baghdad, Rachel had rarely gone outside the walls of Camp

Victory, and even though she still had to wear her vest and carry her M-16 every time she went outside, she was not conducting raids or patrolling dangerous areas of the city. Evan discovered that on this tour she was only in Baghdad from time to time and spent most of her time flying around from camp to camp in Black Hawk helicopters, exposed to far more risk than during her first tour.

Evan tried his best to picture her routine, if she even had one, but he could not see it in his mind. He could envision the helicopter leaving from and returning to the base camp and having to fly low over areas where extremists undoubtedly hid, ready to shoot down any American aircraft. He also tried to picture her traveling the Iraqi countryside very much unprotected and vulnerable. He hated every image that came to his imagination but was powerless to change his reality or hers.

Like before, he tried to think of other things as he lived his days at home, but he could never shake the negative thoughts for long. Both Senator Obama and Senator McCain used the war as a political tool in their campaigns, and periodically, someone in Congress would mention an escalation of forces and attacks, which made Evan even more uneasy.

He felt like his entire life had been put into neutral, and he could never figure out how to put it fully back into gear. He had never been in a situation like he was now in, so he had no previous experience to draw from, which might help him cope. He could talk to Jordan or perhaps even a couple other close friends, but that would be a really big step for him. He couldn't remember a situation where he had not been able to right his own ship, but this was different. He was unsure of how to set his sail, and most days, he honestly didn't spend the effort to put his sail up at all. His world had become his house, his television, and his computer, and he felt like he was wasting each day that he was being given to live.

Hour after hour, day after day, month after month, he was growing older by himself, and with each passing month, as he read each e-mail, he could feel Rachel moving further away from him. It scared him how quickly everything about his life had changed because of a war. He fully understood how powerful separation from a loved one can be, but his understanding brought him no comfort. He was a fixer, a problem solver by nature, but he could not see a solution to what he now faced.

The end of July once again saw Rachel's birthday arrive, and the realities of distance again cheated Evan out of the chance to plan something special for her. Was this the third year in a row she had been out of the country or the fourth? He couldn't even remember the last time they had gotten to share any kind of special day together. Evan did the best he could and again filled a box with things he thought she would like and could use in Iraq. He packed a humorous birthday card in with the snacks, paperbacks, and other items, and he sent it to her. It felt to him more like an obligation than something he wanted to do for the right reasons. He also sent an e-mail birthday wish to her, but he heard nothing back for five days. He later found out that she was several hundred miles from Baghdad on her birthday, only ten miles from the Iran border, and she didn't receive anything he had sent her until she got back to the base camp. He wondered how she had celebrated her birthday and then realized how sick he was of wondering about things like that.

August was more of the same, and Rachel's e-mails were again filled with excitement for all she was getting to see and do. He remembered one e-mail that could have substituted for nearly every other one she had sent him that summer.

Hi, I'm just back at the base for a couple days and wanted to get you and e-mail. I've been all over the countryside here and have gotten to see all kinds of amazing things. I've taken tons of pictures. This job is giving me all kinds of experience that I can bring back after this tour is over, and I can carry it over to the civilian side and make a lot more money doing the same things I'm doing now. It's hotter than hell here, but I'm having fun and learning a lot.

Me

She never mentioned danger in any way. Was that really how it was there for her? He couldn't totally believe that because every day there were still reports of soldiers dying there. He guessed that her omissions of the dangers there were purely for his benefit so he wouldn't worry as much about her. He was relatively sure that Rachel's mom heard the same things he did to help reduce her worry level. He doubted whether her mom believed Rachel's illusion of safety any more than he did, but he figured that it made Rachel feel better, believing that he believed her, so he never questioned what she told him.

The presidential race had greatly intensified, and Evan was caught up in all the campaigning intrigue. He watched both party conventions with great interest and was convinced that Senator Obama was the better candidate. When the primary season began, he had liked what he had heard from Senator McCain, but the conventions had changed that. Evan was convinced that McCain's choice of a running mate was a cheap and superficial attempt to steal voters, who had supported Hillary Clinton and who still appeared angry with Obama that he had not chosen her as his running mate. He could not support anyone willing to treat the highest office in the land with that level of carelessness and selfishness.

As Evan got more interested and involved in the election, he asked Rachel what she and the other soldiers thought about it all. He wondered how much or how little the deployed soldiers actually knew about any of the specifics of either candidate, and he quickly found out that she knew very little about the election and cared even less. He was astounded that soldiers could be content with remaining uninformed about their next commander in chief. He figured soldiers, in a war, even more so than others, would be incredibly interested in who would be making the highest level war decisions for the next four years.

The only explanation he could come up with was that each individual soldier was such a small piece of the entire giant military apparatus that he felt that no matter how the election turned out, his job would still be to simply take orders. Each day for a soldier at war consisted entirely of totally focusing on the immediate mission at hand. There was little, if any, time to think about political candidates, baseball scores, summer at home, or family members.

He decided that he would keep her caught up on the campaign from time to time, but he also learned that he would have to be a bit careful with what he told her because her mom and brother were McCain supporters. He laughed when he thought of her reading conflicting e-mails from home when her political interest level was minimal to begin with. She did tell him that she would get to vote absentee from Iraq, and she was excited to do that. He found out later that she had not voted in the presidential election, but he never found out why. In the end, he theorized that political details and independent thinking were not important factors to those who spent their days taking orders and following instructions.

September brought with it several things that would make a huge difference in Evan's life. The cooler days and nights meant less yard work and mowing, and he knew it would soon be time to prepare for yet another fall and winter by himself. The harvest moons were less than romantic for him, and he was not anxious for the cold weather that lay ahead. In the middle of September, Rachel sent him an e-mail that initially excited him.

Hey, how is everything? I wanted to let you know that I put in for my seventeen-day leave and got it approved for the middle of December. I can go pretty much anywhere in the United States, but I think I want to go to Florida. Since I'm coming back in December, I have no desire to be home in the cold. I want two weeks of sun and beaches and relaxation. You can start looking into flights for you to take, and I'll tell you more when I get it all finalized. I've got some connections through the military that let me get great rates on places to stay all over the country. I've searched several places and found one I like and can afford.

Evan still had no regular job, so going anywhere for two weeks was easily workable for him. He had no boss to ask permission from, and the trip to Florida sounded like fun to him. He was also somewhat nervous. After more than a year in a war zone, dealing with salutes, regulations, bombs, missiles, helicopters, and danger, he wondered if she could return to being a temporary civilian again that quickly. Would they be comfortable together like they had been when they dated, or had time and distance claimed two more casualties? Evan wasn't sure he wanted to know the answer because he thought he already knew what it might be. He sat and composed an immediate reply to her.

Hi, great news about you getting to come back for a couple weeks, and Florida sounds great. It's nice here now, but in December I'll be ready for some warm weather for sure. Where in Florida will we be staying? Will we be in the same place the whole time? It sounds like you have everything pretty much under control, but if you need me to do anything on this end, just let me know. I'm already looking forward to it.

From then on, Evan looked forward to reading her e-mail updates as each piece of the vacation puzzle was put into place. He had no idea what things she specifically wanted to do, so he simply encouraged her as she put the trip together from Iraq and did what he could to help her from home. It was her vacation trip, so things would be however she set them up to be.

Ten days after Evan learned of the Florida trip, he had another birthday. The last two birthdays had been less than memorable, and he had nothing special planned for this one. He had basically quit worrying about trying to make special days special and had grown used to the subtle disappointment that came when one had no one special nearby to share things with. He was now forty-eight years old and spent a considerable amount of his birthday reflecting on what he had, what he thought he had, and what might lie before him. It was quite a collection of thoughts that got mixed together, like a chef experimenting with various ingredients trying to create something delicious. All day long, he stirred and shook those thoughts, but in the end, all he found was a tasteless mess, and he had run out of ideas for things to add that would create the right flavor.

Jordan had remembered Evan's birthday and gave him a call. "Hey, birthday boy. Why don't you hop in your car and get your butt over here. We're grilling burgers, and we want you to join us."

Evan grinned broadly as he listened. "Sounds like a winner. Let me check my schedule and see if I can fit that in."

"Right," chuckled Jordan. "Just get over here. I've already started the grill."

"Okay," said Evan. "On my way." He enjoyed Jordan's family, and the time with them sounded far preferable to another night at home by himself, foolishly trying to lie to himself about how happy and content he was spending his birthday night by himself.

Earlier that day, Evan had gotten an e-mail from Rachel, wishing him a happy birthday. Immediately following that sentence was a paragraph that told him another major purpose of the e-mail.

Hey, happy birthday! Hope you will have or already had a great day. I never know when you get to read the e-mails I send. Everything here is fine, and I'm still keeping very busy. I wanted to let you know that I've asked my mom to come to Florida too and spend at least a week with us there. She was really excited about the idea, and I need you to line up a plane ticket for her when you get yours. You can talk to her whenever you get the tickets so she'll know her flight schedule. Thanks.

Evan tried to decide if that was a good thing or not, but he knew that only time could answer that question. For the past month or so, both Rachel and her mom had been dropping subtle hints to him about how much they missed each other, and Evan now realized that he was perhaps just being let in on a plan that those two had been putting together without his knowledge.

Evan was happy that the army took care of its soldiers and gave them the freedom to choose their own vacation spot on their leaves from Iraq and allowed them to fly for free. He thought it was fitting and logical, but it was also something the military didn't have to do. There would be over 250 soldiers on Rachel's flight from Kuwait to Atlanta, and he considered how many places they would fan out to once they left that hub. Had other soldiers chosen warm beaches over time at home, or were they so anxious to see home that the weather didn't matter?

Evan and Rachel had previously talked about moving to Florida one day. Neither of them liked snow and cold, but it wasn't quite that simple. All their roots were planted in the Midwest, and pulling those roots up would take more than words and daydreams. It was an enticing thought for someday, for retirement time, but not for a while yet. This trip was for Rachel's relaxation, not for a lifetime. It was only two weeks long, and it wouldn't happen for another three months. Evan's immediate reality that morning had been mowing the yard for what he hoped was the final time for the year. Some of the tree leaves were turning, and it would soon be time to trade in his mower for a rake whenever the leaves began to carpet the yard. He still looked for a job every week and still was met with no success, so all his daily thoughts could not remain on a plane trip south that was three months away. About the same time Rachel had first e-mailed Evan about the Florida trip, the US economy dropped into the tank. The largest banks in the country were on the brink of collapse, and the stock market fell to new lows each day. President Bush and his advisors insisted that Congress had to bail them out or it would lead to a worldwide depression. Things got quite chaotic in the midst of the presidential election, and the country as a whole was quite nervous. Needless to say, there was very little hiring happening anywhere as tens of thousands suddenly found their jobs disappearing without warning.

Evan still followed the campaigns with great interest and periodically relayed major news along with his thoughts to Rachel, who was unable to receive many day-to-day political details. The election was seven weeks away, and the intensity of the speeches and the rhetoric captivated him, and he knew he would remain greatly interested through election day and beyond. Evan was also really glad that Jordan's political views matched his own, and he was grateful to have someone to discuss those things with when they got together.

"You got some nice weather for your birthday," exclaimed Jordan.

"Yeah, I did," agreed Evan. "Just think in the middle of December when you're freezing here, I'm going to be sitting on a Florida beach."

Jordan continued. "That's true. Imagine you and Rachel and her mom all walking in the sand. What do you think about having a chaperone?"

Evan paused for a moment before answering. "I'm not sure. It could be a good thing or a bad thing. I can't decide. They haven't seen each other for a long time, and they are very close, so I can understand why her mom wants to see her. That's not an issue. But I haven't seen her either, and it could be harder to get our stuff sorted out with someone else there. I just don't know."

The aroma of the cooking burgers permeated the deck while they sat and talked and Jordan's children played below them in the yard.

"But she won't be there the whole time, right? Just part of it?" continued Jordan.

"Right. She gets there a few days after I do and will stay a week, so Rachel and I will also have a few days alone after she leaves."

"Interesting."

"I think both of them have been planning this for a while now. The first couple e-mails I got from her about this trip never mentioned her mom coming, and then suddenly it was a done deal. Not sure what to think of that. I don't know why they thought they had to arrange all that like it was a secret or something."

"Maybe Rachel didn't think of having her mom come until she decided where she wanted to go for her trip."

"Doubtful. She talks with and e-mails her mom more than she does with me. This was in the works from the beginning. I'd bet on that."

"Sounds to me like you are kind of excited to go down there but not totally."

Evan laughed. "I'd say that's a pretty accurate description. A guy shouldn't be nervous about getting together with his wife, should he? I hate that feeling, but I can't get away from it. I worry that she has changed a lot, and I have no idea anymore what's in her head about the future. Makes me nervous, I guess."

"I think it's good that you have a few days alone together first. You should know how things really are long before her mom gets there."

"Yeah, I thought about that too. We've got so many things to talk about, and I doubt it will take long to find out what she thinks about everything. Part of me dreads some of the answers I think I'll hear though. This whole deployment thing sucks. Before she left, being with her was so easy. Now every day is like a new challenge of some kind."

"What do you mean?"

"Well, I worry about her all the time, and I don't have a steady job. Nobody is hiring anybody, so there are money things. Just keeping up the house can be a deal, but everybody has that. You know like when the basement floods. Things like that. Going to bed by myself every night. I thought I was all done with that when we got married, but that's pretty much all I've done. I hate it. I didn't care about a night or two while she went to drill or a camp or something, but now it's like I'm single again but not really. I can't stand limbo, and that's where I feel like everything is."

"I understand that. I like knowing things too and can't stand wondering or hearing 'maybe' on stuff. Even if I don't like the answer, give me something definite."

"Exactly," agreed Evan. "It feels like I have a million things that are not definite going on at the same time, and it makes me sick sometimes. Makes me mad, really. Now I still have to wait a couple more months before I can figure out what's really going on in her head. Sometimes it feels like I'm chasing the horizon. I can see it and run after it, but no matter what, I can never catch it."

Jordan didn't answer immediately. He went to the grill and flipped the burgers one more time. He added his secret spices to enhance the flavor and looked out into the yard at his laughing children. "Won't be long now. I'm getting hungry."

"Me too," replied Evan as he rubbed his stomach.

A moment later, Jordan began taking all the burgers off the grill. As he filled the plate, he looked at Evan. "No doubt you're in for an interesting trip to Florida. Don't drive yourself crazy for the next two months worrying about it. Whatever's gonna happen will happen, and you can deal with it then. You want to make it work, right?"

"Sure, I do, but I'm not sure anymore that she does," stated Evan as he rose from his seat and went inside to begin his birthday meal.

"It will all work out," reassured Jordan.

"Sounds easy, doesn't it?"

Two hours later, after the burgers had been devoured and several beers had been drunk, Evan decided it was time for him to go home. The late September sun had sunk below the tree line and had disappeared from view. "Thanks for having me over. The food was excellent."

"Happy to do it," grinned Jordan. "You're family here. You know that, right?"

"I know and I appreciate it," replied Evan. "See ya later."

Evan made his way home and spent the rest of his birthday night in his recliner, changing the channels on his television regularly in search of the most mindless shows he could find. At that point, he had had quite enough thinking and wondering and worrying for one day, and for a few hours, he allowed himself to think about nothing in particular. After all, it was his birthday.

CHAPTER 23

The talk at the table was what one would expect from a group on vacation. They talked about beaches and sea shells and sports and souvenirs. Evan had a beer in his hand and two more sitting on the table. The group he had joined was ready to party, and he laughed when David told him, "You'd better keep up or you'll have to go sit all alone again!" Evan knew David was kidding, but he finished the beer he was holding and started on the next one.

Evan felt lucky to have found this group. They were friendly and warm and acted like they had known Evan for years. Two of the couples decided to make their way onto the dance floor, which left one couple, the single woman and Evan, still sitting there. The music blared throughout the club, and the reggae beat was impossible to resist. Each of the four sitting at the table moved to the rhythm, and Evan finally asked Erin, the single woman in the group, to dance. She smiled broadly, took Evan's hand, and they bounced their way to a spot near the band and showed off their best moves.

Evan and Erin finished dancing to their third song, and both had broken a sweat. The band finally took a break, so they returned to the table to rejoin the others. The laughter was plentiful at the table, and Evan appreciated how comfortable they had all made him feel. He sat back and sighed, realizing that he was genuinely having fun, something that had become foreign to him the past couple years. For the next half hour, the conversation at the table was mostly about nothing, but to Evan, it was perfect. Everything in his recent past had been serious, and he relished being able to drop his guard and begin to be himself again. It was a start anyway.

He was beginning to feel the effects of all the beer he had consumed, but that didn't slow him down. He knew he could sleep in the following morning because his plane for home didn't take off until mid afternoon. Eventually, the band began their next set of songs, and now that the dancing ice had been broken, the table again emptied, and everyone returned to the dance floor for more. It felt amazing to Evan to once again remember what it was like to simply relax and enjoy life, and he made the most of the moment.

As Evan danced, he thought for a moment back to that Orlando weekend and the goals he had set for himself. His intentions had been so good when that convention ended. Building on the excitement and the feelings from that weekend, he had planned on building his business to a large level, but life had again gotten in the way. He had been surrounded by helpful, motivated people in Orlando and had gotten caught up in all the positive possibilities. What he had underestimated was the power of the solitary gloom at home and the apprehension he felt regarding his and Rachel's future. All the negatives had beaten the positives into submission, and Evan had finally surrendered, at least for a while.

All that apprehension was behind him now, whether he wanted it to be or not. Here he was dancing and relaxing in a Fort Myers club, and he had made some new friends and had found his smile again. It seemed to him that perhaps he had finally turned a necessary corner in his life, and he could sense a glimmer of genuine optimism in his heart. He knew that tomorrow he would once again return home, but he felt the future this time would be different than before. This weekend had shown him that there was still life to enjoy. In Fort Myers, he had watched hundreds of people living and thriving like he had done for most of his years, and he knew that he had finally stepped onto the right path to do that again.

Everyone in the group at his table had finished dancing and again returned to their seats. Sweat was wiped from brows, and more smiles were shared as everyone sat and rested. It was nearing midnight, and Evan spoke to the entire table. "Well, everybody, I think I'd like to take a walk along the beach. I'm going home tomorrow and want to do that one more time before I head out. I really want to thank all of you for letting me share this night with you. It meant more to me than you can ever know, but now I think it's time for me to take off."

"Are you sure you have to go?" asked one of the wives. "We're not done partying yet. I think the band has another entire set to play."

"You can dance for me," he replied. "I really think I want to go for a walk. Thanks again for letting me join you. I had a great time."

"Good night, Evan," said David as he gave Evan a hearty handshake. "Take care and good luck with everything."

"Good night all," said Evan, and when he rose from the table, he felt a slight tug on his shirt. He turned to see Erin looking up at him, wearing a broad smile.

"Would you like some company on that walk?" she asked him softly. "A night walk on the beach sounds wonderful."

He hesitated for a moment, thought briefly to himself, and then returned a smile of his own, and she knew that she had just gotten her answer. He took her hand, and she rose from her chair, and the two left the noise of the club and traded that for the solace and peaceful waves of a deserted beach. Evan had no idea where the walk might finish, but he was anxious to chase the possibilities.

A full moon shone on the water, leaving streaks of light everywhere it could. The breeze was calm, the temperature was quite comfortable, and there was very little evidence that it had been raining just a few hours earlier. Evan and Erin walked slowly, looking down from time to time, pretending to hunt for shells and sand dollars. The conversation started small and light, with both of them acting a bit nervous and unsure of what exactly to say. Evan knew that a word or phrase could either completely enhance the moment or ruin it, and he seemed a little scared to take that step.

A couple hundred yards down the beach, they stopped and stared out into the water as far as they could see in the moonlight. Erin's brown hair hung on her shoulders, and she stood quietly. She finally took the chance and wrapped her arm inside Evan's. She pressed close to him, and no words were necessary. Evan took her arm in his and smiled at her. He could not imagine a more romantic setting than where they were standing. The laughter at the table and the dancing had all been a prelude to this moment, and Evan was quite happy to be where he was. The waves gently caressed the shore in a steady rhythm that only added to the overall mood. After a couple minutes of standing motionless, Evan turned to Erin and gently kissed her.

Erin did not seem at all surprised by the kiss. She was still pressed tightly against Evan, and his arms were around her. The moon seemed to silhouette them, and a distant observer could be excused for thinking that he was looking at one person. They stood motionless for several seconds, but it seemed a lot longer to Evan. When the hug ended, he spoke first. "Let's walk some more." Erin smiled, and they resumed their stroll along the beach, but this time they walked holding hands, and the pace was very slow. Evan secretly hoped that perhaps slowing their steps could also slow the clock and trick the night into not ending.

When they reached a small pier, they went out onto it and sat, removed their shoes, and let their toes dip into the cool evening water. Erin turned to him and asked him a very direct question. "Do you believe in fate?" She squeezed his hand as she asked the question softly.

The question surprised him a bit, but he instantly knew the direction Erin was leaning, and he could not immediately convince himself that he was ready to walk that road just yet. That wasn't what this weekend was about. He gave Erin a nonverbal indication that he was about to answer her but was forming the right words in his mind. He splashed his feet a little and leaned back, rested on his hands, slowly turned to face her, and began his reply. "There was a time when I believed in fate, but now I don't think I do, at least not completely. Just a few years ago I had believed in it with all my heart, and so I put my heart totally out on the line, but that line got cut and I fell hard. After that, I felt like I had been pretty naive to believe that that kind of fate was real, or if it was real, then it wasn't meant for me." He looked Erin in the eye and smiled. "Maybe that was more than the answer you wanted."

She nodded in an understanding way. "I've been there too, but I guess I'm still an optimist, and I am still hopeful that's it's there, and someone wonderful is out there waiting to find me or be found by me."

Evan answered her as honestly as he could. "I tried like hell to stay optimistic for a long time, but somewhere along the way, a lot of that optimism left me. I'm still looking for it though, and that's part of why I came here this weekend. I think it's working, and you and your friends have helped me more than you know."

Erin smiled broadly at him. "I'm glad."

Evan continued his explanation. "I really enjoy your company, and this night has been very special for me, but I'm going home tomorrow, and you'll be staying here. I have to be honest. The thought of geography and distance standing in the way of a relationship again is more than I care to deal with. I might be ready again for that someday but not yet."

She leaned in and kissed him again. "It's okay. I know exactly what you mean." She took his hand and pulled him up off the pier. "Let's walk some more."

CHAPTER 24

The calendar turned again, and it was now October. The stores were filled with Halloween goodies, and the presidential election was just four short weeks away. The country was still full of restless energy and uncertainty as experts tried to understand and explain the troubled US economy to nervous citizens. Evan still searched halfheartedly for a job, but with the banks crashing and people being laid off by the tens of thousands, he was not optimistic. Jordan was hired by Rachel's brother to redo and repair some pipes and drainage at their house that had been damaged by recent flooding. It was a big job, and it kept Jordan busy for over a month, so he spent a lot of time with Rachel's mom, who was home during the days when Jordan worked there.

Evidently, Rachel's mom was already incredibly excited about her December Florida trip because Jordan told Evan she talked to him about it every day.

"She's right there talking to me every day while I work. It's like everything she thinks about now is Florida and Rachel, and every time she starts talking, she just grins."

Evan's curiosity was definitely piqued, so he prodded Jordan further. "What kinds of things does she talk about? There can't be that much that we'll do down there other than just be tourists."

Jordan laughed loudly. "You think so, huh? She's got it all worked out already. Did you know that you were moving to Florida once

Rachel's tour is over and that her mom was going to come live there with you?"

"What?" exclaimed Evan. "Are you serious? She tells you that?"

"Only every day. It's all she talks about, and she's counting the days. Hell, she's got everything all figured out and talks to me like it has all been decided and is just waiting to happen."

"That's incredible," muttered Evan as he shook his head in disbelief. "It's the first I've heard of any of this. Rachel and I have talked several times about eventually retiring to Florida someday but not yet."

"I'm thinking you might want to be ready for a change in your plans," Jordan mused sarcastically. "Want me to come help you pack?"

"Funny. I guess one of these days I should ask one of them about their grand plan and find out if I'm involved in it somehow. Maybe I'm the guy who stays behind and just cheers them on. That's just amazing news. You're not making this up, right?"

"No. I swear it's true. I hear it every single day I'm over there working."

"Okay, I believe you," answered Evan, finally convinced it wasn't a gag being played on him by his friend. Evan now faced a dilemma. Rachel had never mentioned an impending Florida move or her mom living with them, so he wondered if he should mention to her that he was now aware of the plan. If Rachel and her mom were planning all that without even talking to him about it, he knew he already had part of the answer to the question as to where he stood with Rachel. The Rachel he had dated and married would have never concocted such a scheme without discussing it with him, but he was learning that Rachel the soldier could do that with ease.

An eerie, uneasy feeling began to creep into Evan's psyche, and it chilled him to think his thoughts could be true. He found himself spending many October afternoons sitting in his porch swing, pretending to care about the world around him. In reality, he was analyzing everything about his life and searching for ways to get it back on track. Feeling weak and out of control disgusted him, and he was extremely tired of it. Now on top of everything else, he felt his self-esteem sink even lower when he realized he was apparently a pawn in a plan Rachel and her mom were about to put into action. He rocked slowly in the porch swing and kept trying to see the whole picture of what was happening to him and around him. The more he thought, the more he felt like he was being used, and his anger rose to a level he had not felt in years. If everything that he thought might be true was actually true, he understood that he was living through the beginning of the end of his marriage. He still watched the news but had grown to hate the war, mostly because he felt like it had ruined the life he had known and had previously enjoyed.

He knew there were benefits to deployed soldiers who were married, and since he now questioned everything, he found himself trying to determine if things like separation pay played a part in why he was still even in the picture for Rachel. He couldn't stand the idea of being a pawn in a bigger game that Rachel might be playing, but at the same time, he didn't see any way to change anything. He was stuck. The negative possibilities poured through his mind like a waterfall, and his frustration swelled. As he tried to put the big picture puzzle together, the prospects of his losing the life he had with Rachel now seemed inevitable. Self-doubt consumed him as he tried to think of things he had said or done or had not said or done to change her feelings toward him so dramatically.

Was it because he didn't have a regular job? Surely she had not become that superficial. Money could always be made in a lot of ways. Was it because he was content with the home and life they had before she deployed and she no longer was? There was an endless stream of questions that Evan knew might never be fully answered, but he asked himself the questions anyway, trying his hardest to find the key to the door that would unlock the mystery.

He remembered back to Rachel wanting to retire in Panama after visiting there, and he remembered the plan of buying the resort in Guatemala. He kicked himself for being naïve enough to think that there wouldn't be a new plan after two years in Iraq. The biggest difference this time seemed to be that the plan, whatever it was, had been put together for Rachel and her mom, and he might be left behind.

He thought about talking to Rachel's mom, but he chose not to. Jordan's sincerity had convinced Evan that there was truly a plan, or at least the beginnings of something somewhat concrete, and he decided to let Rachel tell it all to him in her way and on her terms. Part of him really looked forward to that conversation so that he could let her know how little he appreciated being left out of the loop while another part of him dreaded it more than anything because he felt certain that whenever that conversation happened, it could be life changing and, more than likely, in a very negative way.

The porch swing rocked faster as each October day passed, and Evan's emotions churned. It had not been a fun month for him, and it took a very blunt comment from Jordan for him to realize how truly unhappy he was. It was Halloween, and Jordan and Evan again sat and talked in Jordan's shop. After several minutes, Jordan looked him right in the eye and said, "How long are you going to walk around wearing that scowl? It looks like hell and you need to get rid of it."

Evan looked up with a puzzled expression, like he was completely unaware of the unspoken messages his face had been sending out. Jordan laughed and continued, "I think it's decision time for you. You need some honesty so this is one friend talking to another. You can either sit and mope around every day or figure out a way to turn things around and live again."

Evan somehow found a smile. "You're right. I know you're right. I guess I hadn't realized how obvious my emotions had become to you, and if you're seeing it that easily, I'm sure others have been too."

"They see it. They just don't say anything to you about it. I thought it was time."

"I guess it is," concluded Evan. "Time for me to live again."

December and Florida were now things Evan anticipated with the same vigor as a trip to the dentist. He still wasn't sure if all he had perceived and envisioned in his mind were actually impending realities, but his thoughts appeared to be based on enough logic that he believed them. A small piece of Evan's optimism still clung to a hope that once he got to Florida, Rachel would tell him that she still wanted a future with him no matter where they were, but he could never fully convince himself that would happen.

Rachel and Evan continued to trade e-mails a few times a week, and the upcoming Florida trip was the main topic of discussion. Evan knew, or at least he thought he knew, that she was still traveling all over the Iraqi countryside in helicopters and was regularly outside the somewhat safe confines of Camp Victory, but she never mentioned any of that to him. He could never figure out why she had quit sharing her experiences and successes with him since his approval had used to bring her joy.

Evan gave himself a few days' rest from his frustration and worry and did his best to immerse himself in the presidential election. He had gotten onboard the Obama bandwagon several months earlier and was excited to be part of what promised to be an incredibly historic moment in America. The final two days before the election brought a barrage of television coverage, and Evan soaked up as much of it as he could. He had never before been a political man, but he knew this election was special, and he couldn't wait to join millions of other Americans and cast his vote.

He thought back to how he had gotten interested in the campaigns initially, and like everything else in his life at that point, it had started because of the war and Rachel's deployment. A year earlier, he had been channel surfing for Iraq news and had found some on MSNBC. He began watching that channel, and the stories and commentary had held his interest, so he continued to watch. He had found a news source he trusted. He thought the station was thorough in its coverage of Iraq, and it mixed in enough campaign primary stories to get Evan excited about that too. He had watched with great interest hundreds of reports from Baghdad and other Iraqi cities, but now whenever a report came on that dealt with the war, he was just another disinterested viewer waiting for the next story.

He had tried to pass on his election excitement to Rachel through his e-mails, but like nearly everything else, something always got lost in translation. She seemed totally disinterested in the election or, for that matter, anything that happened in his daily routine at home. Their topics of conversations had seriously deteriorated to almost the bare essentials. Whether on the phone or through e-mails, Rachel rarely asked about anything happening at home, and for whatever reason, she chose not to share many details of the things she was doing in Iraq. Evan continued to write and reply but had given up on being excited about anything he read or wrote. All the messages now were about the Florida trip, so he figured as long as he talked about that, they could at least carry on some version of a conversation.

Election day came with great fanfare. Evan had never seen so many people excited about voting, but he was right in the middle of it all. He went to vote before 8:00 AM and had to stand in a twenty-minute-long line. Nobody in line seemed to mind the wait, and as Evan looked at the crowd, he saw smiles everywhere. He thought to himself that this was his country's best strength, a chance to have a say and make a difference as an individual, and he felt proud.

A few days after the election, Evan's networking company had a luncheon that he attended. Everyone was still buzzing with talk of President-elect Obama and what his election could mean for the future of the United States. Jordan rode with Evan to the luncheon, and the two sat and ate and talked with friends. One couple who knew of Evan's upcoming Florida trip asked him the first deployment questions of the day. "So how excited are you to get away and finally get to see your wife again?"

Evan gave them a smile and replied as enthusiastically as he could. "Pretty anxious." That was his entire answer, and he did not elaborate at all. He felt like such a hypocrite that he tried to quickly change the subject, but this time, it didn't work. Others had heard the question and innocently wanted to satisfy their curiosity by hearing more details of the upcoming trip. They too could only imagine how excited Evan must be to be able to see his wife again after being apart for a year and a half. All Evan could do was continue to smile and answer in generalities, but his answers seemed to be good enough because before long, the conversations again returned to networking and building each person's business. Jordan stayed quiet and vicariously endured Evan's struggle with the questions, wanting to help but not knowing what to do.

Thanksgiving arrived quickly. The mower had been put away, and all the fallen leaves had been raked up and disposed of, and now it again was time for the holiday season and all the frills that came with it. Houses and yards were being decorated, and early shoppers filled stores searching for bargains. Evan's only contact with Rachel's mom had been a phone call when he told her the day and time her plane left for Florida. During that same call, she had invited him to again share Thanksgiving dinner with her and Rachel's brother's family, but this time he declined. He wanted to drive to his parents' house this year and spend a few days with them. That was true, but the unspoken truth was that he wanted to save the grand unveiling of Rachel and her mom's hidden Florida plan for when he got face-to-face with Rachel. He thought if he sat and talked with her mom that some of the details would come out inadvertently, and he knew that could open an entirely new can of worms that he didn't want to deal with yet.

Neither Rachel nor her mom had mentioned anything to him yet about moving to Florida for good, but Jordan had told Evan that Rachel's mom still talked to him about it nearly every day while he worked. The intrigue of the details of whatever was being planned at times got the best of Evan, and it took discipline on his part to be able to block it out and think about other things. His plane left in three weeks, so he knew he didn't have to wait much longer to get his answers.

CHAPTER 25

It was time for Evan to pack for Florida, and though packing was usually a simple routine task for him, this time he struggled with how to fill his suitcases. He not only had to pack for himself, but he also had to search through the tubs containing Rachel's things and find civilian clothes for her to wear. All she would have with her when she got off the plane would be army uniforms and BDUs, and those certainly would not be enough for two weeks in Florida on vacation. Evan searched the tubs and found several pairs of shorts, tennis shoes, sandals, and T-shirts for her, and her things nearly filled one large suitcase. He finished packing her things and then placed his clothes, shoes, and other things into a second bag. When he was finished, he had two full suitcases, and he did not look forward to packing that much to the airport and then eventually to the condo, but he had to do it.

His meeting time with Rachel was also an approximate thing. Rachel, and all the other soldiers who came home on leave, knew the day they would leave Iraq, but then the itinerary got a lot less specific. Each soldier flew from Baghdad to Kuwait and then had to remain there anywhere from one to four days before leaving on another plane for America. Evan's arrival time was concrete, but once he got to Florida, he didn't know if she would already be there or if he would be alone for three days waiting for her to arrive. He thought of that while he packed, and he wasn't sure which of those two possibilities he preferred. If she got delayed, it was even possible that Rachel and her mom could arrive on the same day, and he and Rachel would have no time to themselves alone.

Evan called Rachel's mom to double-check that she had her leaving times correct, even though he knew she had thought and talked of little else for the past two months. "Hi," Evan began. "I'm getting ready to head out and just wanted to touch base one more time and make sure you have your leaving time and flight number and all that."

"Oh yeah, I've got it memorized," she laughed. "Have fun and I'll see you both in a few days."

"Okay," replied Evan. "Have a good flight down."

Since Evan had chosen a discount plane ticket, he left at 7:30 PM, and he knew that boarding the plane was just the first part of what would be a really late night. His actual air time flying to Florida would be just under three hours, plus he lost an hour switching from central time to eastern time. Another downside of choosing the discount path was that while he and Rachel were staying in Fort Myers, his plane landed in Clearwater / St. Petersburg, a two-and-a-half-hour drive from his hotel. Factoring in some time retrieving his bags and getting his rental car, the earliest he could imagine finding the condo in Fort Myers was somewhere around 3:00 AM. Just the thought of it made him tired.

He had several options to choose from in regard to parking his car while he was gone. He could have had Jordan take him to the airport and drop him off, leaving his own car in his garage. He could have parked at Rachel's brother's house and had someone there drive him to the airport and then pick him up when he got back. Either of those would have worked well, but he chose the third option, which was to drive himself to the airport, park there, and just pay the fees. It just seemed easier to take care of himself rather than to inconvenience one of the others twice.

It was time to go. Evan stuffed the two large suitcases into his backseat, cranked the radio up, and began the twenty-five-mile drive to the airport. He always enjoyed getting away from home for a while, and he really liked flying, so even though the other end of this trip was like a great scary unknown, he still sensed some excitement building inside him. He never minded looking like a fool as he drove down the interstate singing loudly to the radio in his car. He had the radio set to the local oldies station and laughed at the irony as he sang along with Bill Withers.

Ain't no sunshine when she's gone,
It's not warm when she's away,
Ain't no sunshine when she's gone,
And she's always gone too long
Anytime she goes away
Wonder this time where she's gone,
Wonder if she's gone to stay.
Ain't no sunshine when she's gone
And this house just ain't no home
Anytime she goes away

He reached the airport, picked up his parking stub, and claimed the first empty parking space he saw. The suitcases were bulky, but he got them to the counter and got checked in. The terminal was fairly crowded, and Evan wondered how many others were also headed south to escape the cold. It occurred to him that each person there, whether departing or arriving, had his own issues, his own reasons for being there, and his own life story. For some reason, that thought impressed him and gave him a different perspective on his trip and his own situation. It also steered his thoughts to Rachel and her reasons for whatever plans were in her mind. He hoped that when they got together again, shared memories of their time together would stack up favorably when placed against her new, potentially individual dreams.

After walking through the metal detectors and putting his shoes back on, Evan refilled his pockets with his wallet, money, and his iPod.

He found the correct departure gate, found a seat, and waited. Twenty minutes later, the announcement to board the plane was given. He found his seat and fastened the seat belt, and once he heard the plane engines roaring, he knew the time had really arrived. If Rachel had gotten to leave Kuwait on time, after a year and a half apart, they would again be together in just a few hours.

CHAPTER 26

Once a soldier left Iraq and reached Kuwait, there was no communication with home, so Rachel was unable to call Evan's cell phone and let him know where she was. He also had to turn his phone off during his flight to St. Petersburg and was unable to see if she had left him a message. Evan liked specifics and knowing details, and he realized again how much difficulty he would have dealing with the military and its way of doing things. For him, once something was decided, he processed the information, dealt with whatever the details were, and moved on. He really disliked plans that kept changing, and rearranging "final" plans seemed to be standard operating procedure for the army. Over the years, Evan had seen Rachel receive sets of orders for various assignments, complete with dates and times, only to watch her get revised orders a day or two later and sometimes even a second change following the first one. With that in mind, as he flew in the night toward Florida, he could not even say for sure that Rachel had gotten to Kuwait, let alone boarded her plane to the United States. For all he knew, someone had changed her flight plans, and he would have several days on the Fort Myers beach alone.

Evan's flight was extremely smooth, and he enjoyed his good fortune of not having anyone sit next to him on the plane. He was able to stretch out and really relax, and as usual, when he flew, he took a nap. For some reason, flying in a jet worked like a sedative for Evan, and he found it extremely easy to go to sleep on flights. He woke up when the captain announced that they were preparing to land, and he looked out his window and took in the lights that dotted the ground below.

The plane touched down at the Clearwater / St. Petersburg airport at 11:00 PM, and it only took a few minutes for Evan's bags to appear on the luggage carousel. He hauled them over to the car rental counter to pick up his temporary vehicle, and by the time the paperwork for that was completed and the suitcases were in his car, it was 11:45. Before he pulled out of the parking lot, he turned his cell phone back on, and to his surprise, he had missed two calls during his flight, one from a friend back home and the other from Rachel. He listened to her voice mail and discovered that everything had been on schedule for her and that she was waiting in their condo in Fort Myers. His entire demeanor changed. His casual behavior suddenly disappeared, and all three months of his anxiety about this night returned. He had checked a map before he left home and knew how to get from the airport to Fort Myers, but he had no idea where their condo was, so he called Rachel to find out how to get there.

A groggy voice answered the phone, and he immediately knew he had interrupted her sleep. Evan had figured she would be extremely tired when she arrived because a twenty-hour flight through multiple time zones would take its toll on anyone's energy level.

"Hi," said Evan. "So you made it on time. I'm impressed."

"Yeah, I landed in Fort Myers shortly after your flight took off." With the military, Rachel had gotten to not only choose her vacation city, but she could also pick a flight that took her directly to wherever she wanted to go. Evan envied her not having to make the long drive following the flight just to get where she was going, and he figured she had already been asleep for at least an hour or two.

"Sorry to have to wake you up. I know how to get to Fort Myers, but I have no idea where the condo is."

"It's fine," she explained. "I knew you'd have to call for directions. Do you have something to write with?"

"Yep. Fire away." She had written the directions to the condo on paper, and she read Evan the directions and landmarks to look for in order to get there. He hoped she had been alert enough to read him the instructions correctly.

"I've still got a long drive ahead of me. Why don't you go back to sleep, and I'll just knock on the door when I get there and you can let me in."

"Okay," she said simply. "Going back to sleep will be easy." With that, the call was over.

He put his phone on the passenger seat and drove out of the airport parking lot. He, too, was already tired, but he knew he could find the energy for the two-and-a-half-hour drive. He always enjoyed new things and new places and was sorry that it was midnight and couldn't see it all. The parts of Tampa Bay that he could see were lit up brightly, and the night air was relatively warm when Evan compared it with the cold he had left just a few hours earlier. Once he left the immediate St. Petersburg area, the scenery could have been that of anywhere in America. It was two hours of nighttime interstate driving with only sporadic other traffic to contend with.

Mile after mile, he knew he was getting closer to being face-to-face with Rachel, and a level of nervousness began to swell inside him. The thousands of things he had thought and wondered over the past eighteen months were again brought to life, and whatever sleepiness he had felt earlier was gone. He sighed and swallowed hard when he saw the Fort Myers exit he needed to take, and once he got off the interstate, he grabbed the directions he had gotten from Rachel and began his search for the condo.

Evan looked at the clock in the car as he drove through Fort Myers for the first time in his life, and it read 2:50 AM. He yawned but still didn't really feel tired. He knew the condo was just off the beach, but so far all he had seen was city. There was not even a hint of water yet, but he knew it had to be nearby.

He thought he had made all the correct turns but felt completely lost until he saw a sign that said "FT MYERS BEACH 2 MILES." He felt momentary relief that he was almost there, but along with the relief came great anxiety. Just a couple more miles and he would see his wife for the first time in a very, very long time, and he had no clue what would be said or what each of them would feel. He would have never admitted it to anyone else, but he was scared.

Finally he saw the water, and even at 3:00 AM, he could tell the Gulf was impressive and immense. Amazingly, there was still activity on the sidewalks and the roads, and Evan couldn't help but wonder if those people were really early risers or partiers, who had not made it home yet. From the landmarks Rachel had given him in her directions, he knew he was less than a mile from her, and as every second passed, he felt more and more that his heart was going to jump out through his throat.

He soon saw the sign and the marquis for their condo, and he eased the car onto the property. He drove around, eyeing the room numbers on the doors until he found the right one. He found a parking spot, pulled in, and turned the engine off. Then he just sat, staring blankly at the door. He was less than forty feet from his wife now, and he should have felt uncontainable excitement. Instead he felt nothing, not enthusiasm or dread or nerves—nothing.

He knew he would have to wake her up for the second time in order to get into the room, and he didn't look forward to that. Once he talked his feet and legs into moving, he got out of his car and pulled out the suitcases. He shut the car doors as quietly as possible out of simple courtesy for all the others there who were surely asleep, and he began walking toward the door.

Would she be excited to see him? He wished he knew a lot more of what she was thinking, but he didn't, and that made him again feel somewhat helpless. Based on her mom's constant words to Jordan, he knew for certain there was a plan of some kind, and it had always frustrated him not to be included. It was time for that mysterious curtain to be pulled back and have the answers revealed, and even though he might not like the answers, he knew he would soon have them.

He reached the door and set the suitcases down, and then he just stood there for a few seconds. There had been so much anticipation for this moment, both good and bad, and now it was here. Every answer regarding his future lay just on the other side of the door, and he hoped he was ready for whatever those answers might be. With more courage than he thought it would require, he raised his hand and knocked on the door. After a few seconds, he heard stirring in the room, and eventually the door opened and there she was.

CHAPTER 27

Evan smiled at the condo door when Rachel opened it and looked at him while wiping the sleep from her eyes. He could tell that she was not even close to being fully awake as she stood in the doorway in her army T-shirt.

"Hi," said Evan fairly quietly. "Sorry to have to wake you again."

"It's fine," she replied.

Once inside, Evan closed the door behind himself, and at long last, they were alone in the same room. Oddly, as soon as Rachel saw it was Evan, she turned around and walked back into the bedroom. He could see part of the kitchen and living room because Rachel had left the entry way light on. The bedrooms were around a corner and still in darkness, so he had no idea what they looked like yet. He now stood in the hallway alone. They had exchanged a simple hello, and then she really had retreated back to bed. He knew she was extremely tired, and his trip had been only a fraction of what her trip had been, so he gave her the benefit of the doubt.

He had pictured at least a dozen different ways their first moment might go, but at no time had he imagined what had just happened. Just two words uncluttered with any emotion or smile did nothing to lessen his anxiety regarding the next two weeks. It also left him wondering what to do next. Should he join her in the bedroom and wake her up for the third time that night? Should he just toss the suitcases in the living room and sleep on the couch? Should he take the second bedroom so they could each sleep as long as they needed to in order to be energetic the next day? He had been with her for less than five minutes, and he already felt confused and alone. He was not excited about what the sunshine would bring in a few hours.

He left the suitcases where they were and went out onto their deck. Even in the middle of the night, the Florida air felt good to him, and he sat in a full-length lawn chair and checked out what scenery he was able to see in the dark. Their condo was across the street from the beach, but it didn't matter. It was still soothing to him, so soothing in fact that before he realized it, his heavy eyes had closed and he was asleep in the chair on the deck. Evan was awakened four hours later by workers beginning their morning routines. He heard them trimming shrubbery and hosing down the cement by the pool, and there were other various chores going on around him. When he opened his eyes, it took a few seconds for him to remember where he was, and when he realized fully, he sat up and looked inside to see if Rachel had gotten up yet. She had not.

The chair and the damp night air had stiffened his muscles and joints, and he was forced to rise slowly from the chair. He lumbered inside and hoped he would find a coffee pot. He was pleased to see that the resort had provided both a pot and a complimentary supply of coffee for their use. When the coffee was made, he poured a cup, and it immediately made him feel better and at least somewhat awake. He wondered to himself how long that good feeling would last.

He took his coffee into the living room and turned on the television just loudly enough so that he could barely hear it. It was a little over a month after the election and a month or so before the inauguration of President-elect Obama, and Evan had become fascinated by the transition process of the two administrations. He did not know what Rachel had planned for the day, but he felt confident that it did not involve sitting in front of the television watching political news, so he thought he would hear what he could while he could.

Evan finished the entire pot of coffee and had made another one before he heard any movement in the bedroom. He checked his watch, and it was nearly 11:00. The sun was shining brightly outside, but he still sat on the couch in the clothes he had worn the day before. A few minutes after he heard movement in the bedroom, Rachel emerged, looking alert and much fresher than she had looked in the middle of the night. She rubbed her eyes when she saw Evan sitting on the couch and asked him, "What time did you get here? I barely remember opening the door for you and have no idea what time it was when I did that."

Evan answered her nonchalantly, "About 3:00." And as he answered, she too made her way to the coffee pot for her first cup of the day.

It was immediately clear to Evan that there was an unspoken distance between them that had never existed before her deployment. There was no hug or kiss with the greeting, just a casual and unfeeling question that could have been exchanged by two strangers passing each other on the street. Evan had a good idea how everything there would go even before Rachel had taken her first sip of coffee.

She took her coffee out onto the deck, passing Evan in the living room without saying a word. He decided to join her there, partly because the day was so beautiful and partly because they had a thousand things to talk about, and he was ready to get that started. He again sat in the chair that had been his bed overnight, and he was a little surprised that since she knew he had arrived during that night that she had not even asked him where he had slept. He would soon come to understand that his sleeping spot would only be the tip of the iceberg of her indifference toward him.

This was her first morning on American soil in a year and a half, and he was curious how that felt to her. She was once again seeing all the American conveniences and excesses that are taken for granted by those of us who never leave the country. "So, what's it like to see America again?"

She replied quickly. "I don't honestly know how it feels, but in a way it feels like coming home, and that always feels good." Evan silently wondered if she really believed that truly coming home, to their house, would feel equally good to her.

They were both hungry and in need of a shower, and Evan decided to go first. He told Rachel her clothes were in one of the suitcases, and he hoped he had packed things she would want to wear there. Before Evan went to take his shower, she went through all the clothes he had brought for her and only took some of the things out. "Some of these things I probably won't wear," she explained. I figured I would shop here and buy some new shorts and capris to wear."

Evan grinned a little. "That's totally up to you. Everything came out of your closet, and I just took a shot at what you'd want." With that, he marched to the shower.

He was happy to be clean and to have on fresh clothes. He was also ready for some food and eager to explore the beaches of Fort Myers. Rachel showered next, and when she was done they headed out to get some food. They each had a rental car so there was a momentary pause as they decided which car to take. Rachel had rented a sports car and she spoke up first. "Let's take mine. I want to drive it some more. It's fun." Evan climbed into the passenger seat, and they were off.

Lunch was a burger at the beach, and the conversation was entirely superficial, like two former friends reacquainted once again. There were plenty of topics of real substance that needed to be talked about, and they both seemingly knew it might not all be pleasant once that began, so it appeared that neither one wanted to open that Pandora's box just yet. They chose an open-air restaurant and were able to view the anxious tourists rushing to claim their spots in the sand.

"So you really go all over the country in helicopters?"

"All the time. Those things are amazing," she replied in between bites.

"Don't you worry about someone shooting them down?"

"Not really. If we thought about that all the time, we'd never get anything done."

"I guess that's right. I just can't imagine though."

A young couple passed them while walking briskly, both of them covered in tattoos that were totally on display around their swimsuits.

Evan just shook his head. "Look at those two. Why would you do that to yourself, especially at that age and then have to sport those the rest of your life? I don't get it."

"That's a little excessive," she answered. "But I see tats all the time over there, and they aren't so bad. I like them."

"I don't get it, I guess."

"It's their bodies. They can do with them what they want."

"That's true," replied Evan. "Better them than me. I think it looks like awful."

After the hamburgers were finished, they walked together around the corner and got their first full look at Fort Myers Beach. Since it was now early afternoon, the beach was quite crowded. The sun baked the snowbirds, who lay motionless on their towels, and children bounced up and down in the cool, shallow water and then ran cheerfully back to smiling parents. Sand castles had been constructed and destroyed and then rebuilt up and down the beach.

Evan and Rachel were in their swimsuits, and they placed their towels on one of the empty spaces on the sand. Evan had left the cold of the Midwest while Rachel had come from the desert, so the eighty-five-degree heat seemed different to each of them. The biggest difference for Rachel, even though she had endured temperatures over 110 degrees, was that here, she did not have to be in uniform and could relax as a very temporary civilian. For Evan, it was simply a welcome heat wave and an amazingly nice change from the twenty-degree temperatures he had left behind at home.

The two spent three hours lying on the beach and wading in the water and then decided to drive around and explore the area more fully. The beach was great, but they both knew there would be many more places to see and things to do. They got back into the sports car and found their way to Sanibel Island, crossing a long impressive bridge to get there. There was a toll booth that had to be driven through prior to entering the island, and it cost six dollars to drive into Sanibel. Rachel showed the attendant her military ID, and the fee was waved. She grinned and drove on.

Once on the island, they both became full-fledged tourists, checking out shops and sights as they came to them. Everything was new and beautiful and quite unlike the places they had both recently left. Evan was definitely not used to things being green and in full bloom in mid-December, and the thick, abundant foliage was a welcome change from the Iraqi desert, where Rachel had spent so many straight months. They drove most of the entire length of Sanibel Island and eventually reached Bowman Beach. Rachel parked the car, and another round of beach exploration and shell hunting began. Evan laughed out loud at the sign of beach rules that was posted. The fourth rule on the list was "No Nude Sunbathing." "I wonder if they've had a lot of trouble with that one."

Rachel loved to collect shells, so she showed some excitement to begin doing that, and even though Evan did not share her passion for that, he walked with her up and down the beach while she added to her collection. The two talked about everything and nothing at the same time, and eventually they both sat down in the sand. They began with discussion of flights and Kuwait and some of her work in Iraq, and then the conversation returned to the present. "Do you have all the things you want to see and do here all figured out?" inquired Evan.

Not really," she said. "I've researched a few things about the area, but mostly I just want to play it by ear. I thought it might be fun to drive around and see some of the other towns in the area once Mom gets here, but mostly I don't have things planned at all."

Evan saw his opportunity, and he took it. "Since you brought up your mom, there are some things we need to talk about that deal with her."

"Like what?" Rachel asked. "She's only going to be here for part of the time that we're here."

"Oh, I know. It's not that. It's totally something else.

"Okay. What is it?"

"She has been very busy talking to others back home about Florida and her future and our futures here. Apparently as soon as this tour is finished for you, we're all three moving down here together, and she's going to live with us. Where do you suppose she came up with that story?" Evan left off there, anxiously waiting for the answer to his question.

Rachel immediately stopped picking up shells and got a somewhat defiant look on her face. Evan could tell she was formulating her thoughts before she responded. He had seen that look before, but it had been a long time. After a few seconds of really uncomfortable silence, she started her answer. "Mom and I have talked some about moving to Florida permanently to get out of the cold. Nothing definite has been planned, but we thought it would be fun to scout out some possible places while we were here. That's all."

Evan tried to sarcastically smile, but his attempt came across more as the look of a man who fully knew he was being patronized and told half the story. He was sure his answer to Rachel was as sarcastic as his smile when he said, "You should probably tell her that nothing is definite then because for six weeks she has been excitedly telling lots of people that it's a done deal as soon as you get home for good. The strangest part of the whole thing is that she has been telling a lot of people that story but has never once talked about it with me. Never even mentioned it. Don't you think that if I'm supposed to be moving that I should at least be let in on some of the details?"

Rachel had been confident in her first answer, but Evan's last statement had removed some of that confidence although it did nothing to lessen her defiant tone. The real discussion had only begun. Her next response created an equally defiant glare on Evan's face, but it was the statement he had waited over a month to hear.

"Look. Mom has lived with my brother for several years now, and I'd like to have her with me for a while."

The "me" in her answer pierced him like broken glass, and Evan responded quickly. "Have her with you? You? You mean have her with us right?" He then posed to her what he thought was a very simple question. He had looked in her eyes and coldly asked, "Since you and I have been apart for the better part of two years, don't you think it might be a good idea for us to get to know each other again before inviting anyone else to move in with us? When were you and your mom going to let me in on this plan? Try and guess how fun it has been hearing all this crap from others and not having a clue what the hell they were talking about."

Suddenly every sound on the beach could be heard because it was absolute silence between Evan and Rachel. For several seconds, the world was waves charging and retreating; seagulls sprinting to and fro, competing for food; and the sounds of the ceaseless breeze across the beach. He could see the irritation in Rachel's eyes, but he did not speak. However, after another silent minute, Rachel finally did.

"I've got obligations to my mom, and I want to take care of her. It's not just up to my brother and his family to do that. What if your parents needed a place to live? Would you just turn them out somewhere?" Once she opened the faucet of her emotions, the words continued to flow. "And what the hell is up with you not having a job yet? For over two years? I can't support everybody from thousands of miles away in a war. What do you do every day?" She sat facing the water and only occasionally glanced at Evan as she vented for all she was worth. Evan also sat staring at the water and never interrupted her. He felt smaller with every sentence she spoke, but what she failed to ever realize was that what he felt at that moment was close to what he had felt every day at home for the past year and a half. There was nothing new, and Evan's self-esteem was so low anyway that he just sat for the moment and quietly took everything Rachel dished out to him. He had wanted answers as to what Rachel was thinking and feeling, and he was getting those answers from both barrels of her verbal gun.

There was sharpness and coldness in her voice that Evan had never heard before, and though he had half expected an exchange like this, he still felt uneasy. Her words to him were blunt and unfeeling, and to Evan, it seemed that she almost enjoyed being condescending with the things she said to him. Evan wondered to himself how many times she had rehearsed this barrage of superiority in Iraq because it was flowing from her lips smoothly. When she finally finished, she looked at Evan and asked "Well, what do you have to say?"

Instead of answering her right away, he slowly got to his feet, brushed the sand from his hands and his shorts, and looked as far out over the water as he could. When he was ready to speak, he turned and looked into his wife's cold eyes and simply said, "Your mom has been telling the truth, hasn't she? You two have it all neatly worked out for the both of you. What do I have to say? I say I hope you two are very happy together because I've had more than enough of others dictating my life. I'm not a soldier under your command. That's not how a marriage works, or have you been away from me so long that you've forgotten? I think we should go back to the condo." He looked at her with a calm, cool smile and said, "That's all I've got to say for now." He then began walking by himself back to the car. He never looked back once to see whether or not she was following him.

Everything that Evan had feared and imagined since September was happening right before his eyes. He hated that his intuition had been right. Something had told him their reunion would go like this, and he believed his reaction to her words had puzzled her. How could she have ever guessed that what had just happened on the beach had been played out in similar forms in Evan's mind dozens of times? Evan stood quietly beside the car and waited, and when Rachel got there, they climbed in and shared a very uncomfortable twenty-minute ride. It was early evening, and the Fort Myers nightlife was just beginning to get underway. People lined the sidewalks, and music rang out from clubs attempting to draw people inside. Things were far less than festive in their car, and after she parked it, she went to their room, but Evan went the other direction and sat in a lawn chair near the swimming pool. He mentally ran through several options that he could take next, and he knew his choice would be a major one, so he thought carefully. After fifteen minutes of contemplation, he made his decision, and he pulled out his cell phone.

CHAPTER 28

E van sat by the pool and dialed the number of the airline he had flown down on, and after jumping a few telephone switchboard hoops, he finally spoke with an actual person. He spoke in generalities to the operator regarding his reasons, but he wanted to know if he could switch his return flight to something much sooner than the one he currently had, which was sixteen days away. Less than twenty-four hours into his "vacation," he was ready to leave and go home. He found out that he could change his ticket to a flight leaving the following afternoon, and he told the operator on the line, "I'll get back with you soon and let you know for sure."

Most of the negatives he had imagined regarding Rachel and his marriage had come to pass on the Sanibel Island beach, and he didn't know if there was a fix. He wanted no part of two more weeks of tension and feigned fun in Florida, so he had decided to let Rachel and her mom have total freedom to do whatever it was they had been planning to do without him. For the most part, he would not even need to repack his suitcase if he left the next day, and his biggest worries at the moment were his next conversation with Rachel and the night hours that lay ahead. He wasn't sure when or how he would tell her he was thinking of leaving early, but he doubted his decision would upset her much.

Evan remained at the pool a while longer and watched with jealous eyes as families laughed and played together in the warm water. He hated being miserable so often, and he resented the war and the army more at that moment than he ever had before. He knew he was being selfish, but he also knew his world had perhaps just changed forever on that beach, and there was no remedy that he could think of. He and Rachel had never really argued in all the time they had been together, and the Rachel he had known three years earlier could have never spoken like she had done an hour earlier.

He did not understand all the ways a war and being away from home can change and affect a person, and he knew he would never fully know; but at the same time, he wanted someone to know that the separation also affected those at home too, even though that rarely, if ever, got any attention. How could he ever explain to Rachel or anyone else the odd mix of emotions that raced through him every day that she had been away from him? Pride, anger, selfishness, and loneliness are rarely thrown together at the same time, and when he added his guilt for not having a regular job, it quite often overwhelmed him. The part that hurt the most though was that Rachel had never asked him, not even once, how he felt about anything having to do with her deployment. At this point, all Evan could do was surmise that whatever he felt did not interest or matter to her any more. She had her plans and her job, and he believed she could never again feel as much at home with him as she did in her uniform when surrounded by the other soldiers. If he would have had a white flag, he would have taken it up to their condo and officially surrendered.

As the sun began to set over the Gulf, Evan forced himself out of his chair and began walking back to their room. He had no idea what Rachel had been doing since their return from Sanibel, but he knew that she had not come and checked on what he had been doing. He wondered if her demeanor had calmed or if she had been preparing a second round for him. He honestly didn't care either way at that moment. While he sat by the pool, he had fully grasped what he thought awaited him in the coming months and perhaps years, and mostly what he had envisioned was being alone, not temporarily this time but permanently. If someone could have offered him magic words or a magic sentence to change things, he would have paid dearly to possess them, but he knew that was fantasy.

There was still more to be said than had been said on the beach, pleasant or unpleasant, so he headed toward the door, hoping to find a relatively civil battlefield on the other side. When he unlocked the door and walked inside, he saw Rachel sitting on the deck, busily typing on her laptop. He grabbed something to drink and then turned on the television. He decided to wait a bit to test her mood before the inevitable fireworks began. There was a special on that dealt with the crashed economy and its effect on retailers across the country during the holidays. Evan had tried to explain to Rachel what the US economy had become, but he wondered if she could really grasp the severity of everything during her two-week stay in civilian life. He doubted it, but he turned the television up louder so she could hear everything that was said. When she had left for her first tour, times were good, and as a couple, they had been doing quite well financially and emotionally. There was plenty of money for the mortgage and nice vehicles and basically whatever else they wanted to do for fun. That was not the case now, and it had been another source of the tension between them.

Their networking business was still in its infancy despite their initial big goals, and it had not yet replaced Evan's teaching salary. That had been their original plan, and he was keenly aware every single day that he had not held up his end of the deal. He didn't think he could ever explain his lack of energy or ambition or desire to Rachel, so he had never really tried. He had figured that any explanation he could give would make him sound like a whiner.

Rachel typed on her laptop throughout the entire holiday special, and the two had not yet spoken a word since they left the beach. Surely she did not want two weeks of this any more than he did, but he could not be sure of that. Perhaps she had been waiting to be face-to-face before she truly let him know how she felt. He could relate to that because he had done the same thing, and when the television special ended, he walked out onto the deck and asked her calmly, "What are you so busy with?"

She didn't look up for her laptop. "Work stuff. I left in the middle of a project in Iraq, and I still need to keep up with it, even on vacation."

Evan was sure that was true, but he also thought her typing was just another chance for her to contrast how busy she was with how busy he wasn't. "I also got an e-mail from Mom. She's chomping at the bit to get down here."

Evan continued. "Maybe you should change her plane ticket and move it up a couple days to get her here sooner."

The typing suddenly stopped, and for the first time she looked directly at him. "Why would I do that?"

"Several reasons. The first one is that she can't wait to get here, and you want her here just as much. The second one is that I don't think you care one way or the other whether I'm here or not. Why did you bring me here? From what I've seen so far, I think it was more out of a sense of obligation than because you really wanted to be close to me again."

"Obligation?" she questioned.

"Yeah. How would it look to everyone if they all knew you were home on your vacation from war and didn't spend that time with your husband? That would start all kinds of questions, wouldn't it? Gotta keep up appearances, don't we? Look, we've been apart for a year and a half, and now we've been together for nearly a full day, and we haven't even physically touched once. I don't think you give a shit whether I'm here or not. It's like old college buddies getting together and sharing a place for a while before they again go their separate ways."

Evan didn't stop there. "This is your trip and your time. I came here as optimistic as I could be, hoping that this would be a great chance for us to rediscover each other and remember how everything felt between us not that long ago. I wanted that so much, but how can I be optimistic about any of that now?"

"I don't know. I've thought about all this too, hoping there might be something there when we both got here."

"And?" questioned Evan with an equal amount of anticipation and dread as he waited for the answer.

"It's not there. Sorry if that sounds cold, but it's not there."

"You feel nothing? Damn, that's unbelievable," shouted Evan. "That had to be decided in your head long before you got here. I was such a naive fool thinking there was even a chance when I came here."

"Why don't you have a job yet?" she said out of the blue.

"So that's it? That's the big turnoff? What a joke. That's not a reason. That's just a convenient excuse that makes whatever your real reasons are easier to live with. I've tried to explain that to you several times, but you either didn't want to hear the reasons or you didn't believe them when I told you. That's another reason why I think I should go back home early. I have no desire to listen to how worthless and unproductive I am for another two weeks."

"I'm sure that's true," said Rachel confidently. "You're not worthless. I've never said that, but come on. Over two years with hardly any income. What the hell have you been doing?"

"You've never said it directly, but you've indirectly said it a hundred times. What have I been doing? I've mostly been trying to figure out how best to be supportive to you and keep everything going back home. You do remember home, right? In case you've forgotten, I have traded three years of my life for your military service too. You were the one in the other countries, but trust me, my fears and emotions were in those countries with you every single day. Every bombing, every soldier's death, and every rocket that was launched took a piece out of me because I knew I could lose you at any time. I wonder if that ever even occurred to you."

"So you sat home and worried all the time?" she inquired. "I kept telling you that I was fine and relatively safe. How long did you plan on doing that?"

"Until you came back for good, I guess," Evan answered. "I don't know. I felt trapped. Still do. I knew every day I needed to be doing more, but it wasn't that simple."

"You were never like that before I left," Rachel continued. "You always had a job and had tons of things going on. What happened?"

"What happened?" asked Evan. "You don't know? You happened. The military happened. Panama happened. Guatemala happened, and then Iraq happened. Think about it for a second. I saw you more when we were single. Back then, most of the things in my life were within my control. Now it's like nothing is controllable. It's all out of my hands, and everything that happens is decided by either you or the army, and that's a pretty damned helpless feeling. Even this trip was out of my hands. You decided when and where, and your money got me here and so on. I am not very good at living like that, and if you want to know the truth, somewhere along the line while you have been in Iraq, I guess I just basically gave up and said the hell with it. I'm not proud of that, but there it is. You haven't said or written one warm or romantic thing to me in over a year, so I have to think that you've been gone so long that you've forgotten everything you ever even liked about me, and after all this time, we finally get to be in the same place, and all you can tell me for an explanation is 'it's not there.' Wow!"

"I feel like I've been doing everything for both of us, and I'm tired of that," she explained. "I can't get ahead doing that."

"I'm sure you do feel that way," Evan stated. "Trust me, I know. I think how different all this would have been if you were home more than 20 percent of the time. And don't kid yourself anymore. You haven't been doing everything for us. You've been doing everything for you."

"You knew that my being gone was always a possibility."

"Yeah, but not this much. I wasn't ready for being alone again all the time. I thought I could handle it all. I thought we could both handle it all and keep things together no matter what, but I was wrong."

"I love what I'm doing, and I'm not going to stop. There's a big world out there, and I want to see lots of it."

"I understand that, and I'm sure you're very good at everything. Have you ever once even thought about the cost of you seeing the world and being gone all the time because the cost is pretty high. We had a world at home too, and I liked it. I honestly don't think you even remember the things you used to feel about home or me. So now what? Do you still want to be married, or am I holding you back there too?"

Rachel did not immediately reply, which to Evan was very disturbing. After a few seconds, she looked down at her laptop again and quietly said, "I don't know. I really don't."

"Well, isn't that outstanding," he exclaimed in frustration. "Why did you have me come here? It really was just to keep up appearances, wasn't it? I guess you can let me know when you decide for sure and make it 'official' whether you think you still want a husband or not. I need to get out of here for a while. I'm going to go get some food. I'd ask you to join me, but I'm sure you're still busy with your project."

"Go ahead. I'll be here," she replied. "I'm not hungry."

Evan walked quickly out of the condo. It didn't matter to him where he went to eat as long it was somewhere other than where he was. Before Evan started the engine, he just sat in his car like he had done the night before when he was summoning the courage to face Rachel for the first time. This time he sat there with different thoughts, none of them good ones. It was as if he was waiting for Rachel to come charging out the door and ask for him to stay, but after a moment, he wanted to kick himself for thinking that because after the exchange they just had, he knew that wouldn't happen. When his temporary illusion ended, he slammed his hand on the dashboard and started the engine.

He was so used to eating alone that doing it one more time seemed somehow normal. He knew it was not normal though, and his frustration built on the way to his meal. The whole situation mystified him. As he drove down the beach road, he wished he could get inside Rachel's mind so he could know what she was thinking. Evidently, while in Iraq, she had spent more time than he had imagined, thinking and stewing and brooding over the things he was either doing or not doing at home. Had she decided six months ago that she was angry or disappointed with him? Had it been a year or more? He had seen no evidence of her dissatisfaction prior to her deployment, but she was good at hiding her emotions so he couldn't be sure. He finally realized that he had greatly underestimated the level of restlessness that lay within her.

Looking back, there were subtle signs that she had changed after her trip to Panama. There were more changes after her six months in Guatemala, but overall, she had still been the Rachel he had fallen in love with. The changes included very different eating habits, more frequent use of rough language like soldiers in the field would use, and a lot more of her leisure time was spent on military things rather than on some of the things they had enjoyed and shared before she had gone on her trips. She was also more abrupt and to the point and very businesslike in her conversations and in the way she handled issues that arose. Things that used to be fun for her and would make her laugh had seemingly become far less important to her. He wondered to himself when the laughter inside her had died, and it made him very sad that it had.

He could at least partially understand how all that could happen to a soldier far from home and in a dangerous situation every day. Day-to-day joy and laughter would surely be at a premium when one had to be constantly on guard, protecting his own life and the lives of his fellow soldiers. Laughter and smiles had become equally rare for Evan at home but for far different reasons. Laughing together with Rachel had used to be a daily activity, but now Evan feared that their days of shared joys of any kind were gone.

It was time to eat, and he walked into one of the restaurants near the main beach and found an empty stool at the bar. He was more than ready for a beer, so he ordered one and looked at a menu. He read the choices for a couple minutes and then decided he would keep it simple and just have a hamburger and fries. He had become a veteran of sitting by himself and calling a hamburger a meal, and he thought he would do it one more time.

Two hours and five beers later, Evan decided to leave and return to the condo. He was pleased the drive to the condo was less than two miles and had no turns, for his senses had been somewhat dulled by the beer he had drunk. As Evan neared the door to the condo, he felt like a gambler, who had gone all in drawing to an inside straight while Fate sat across the table laughing at him, holding a flush. He knew the odds of winning or even surviving the hand were long, but he was committed to the pot and decided to play it out. He also knew he could still leave his plane ticket at its original departure date, and when he went inside, he held out one last hope that Rachel would give him a reason to do that and to stay.

That hope quickly faded into the silence of the condo. Two of the lights were on, but there were no sounds, and Rachel still sat in front of her laptop typing. Evan rejoined her on their deck and sat down. "Still at it, huh?" he began.

"Yeah. I have a lot to do."

"I bet you're tired. I'm sure your body is still on Baghdad time, isn't it? And you have to still have some jet lag going on."

"I'm getting tired, but I'll be fine," she explained. "How was your food?"

"It was food. Nothing special."

If he had felt much optimism prior to reaching the condo, none of it remained. Rachel's effort level toward him when he sat down was zero, and he knew his effort toward her had been only marginally higher, and that combination was not a recipe for any kind of success. He was closer to giving up his marriage than he had ever been before, and once again Evan the problem solver had run out of solutions. He looked out at the busy street that buzzed in the Florida darkness, people hurrying somewhere to do something, and he knew it was his turn to go somewhere and do something too. "So did you change your mom's ticket?"

"Actually, I did. She was already packed anyway, so she was more than ready to come early and stay longer," laughed Rachel.

Evan sat for a second watching her. "It's nice to hear you laugh. I've missed that too. A lot. I told you she was ready to get here. I guess I should call the airline and get my ticket changed too."

"If you want. You're welcome to stay too," she stated.

"Why? Would you like me to stay?"

"It's already paid for. You can if you want."

"Wow! Because it's paid for? You can't even tell me that you want me to stay, can you? I guess you're still deciding. I appreciate the generous offer, but I think I'll go back home to the world I know. That way you and your mom can do whatever it is you've been planning without having me here in the way. I'll take the spare bedroom tonight." With that, he made his way inside. It was one of the longest short walks he could ever remember. Evan lay in the bed and cried for the first time in a very long time. He cried for wasted time and for dreams and goals that would never come to pass.

CHAPTER 29

Morning arrived, and once again, Evan was the first one awake. He made some coffee, took a shower in the second bathroom, and made sure the few things he had unpacked were placed back inside his suitcase. He stepped onto the deck and called the airline. He was pleased that he could still change his return flight to that afternoon and was tempted to leave right then and drive to St. Petersburg, but he decided to wait a little longer for Rachel to wake up. The morning sunshine on the deck was quite warm, but after an hour, Evan had had enough and was ready to leave. He went inside and found some paper, and though he knew a note was a cowardly way to say something, he began writing.

I'm going home. You remember that place, don't you? The house we shared—the place where we laughed and loved. It's obvious to me that your new home is the army and the joy it seems to bring you. I don't know how to compete with that, and I never thought I would have to. Even if I knew how, I'm not sure that I could offer you enough to compare with where you've been, what you've seen, and the things you have done in uniform, and I've very sorry for that. I feel like I mostly did my best to support you and all the things you wanted to do with your military career, but I know that distance and time have finally beaten us. I also know this is not a game, though sometimes it feels that way. We were both always too busy worrying about stepping on the other's feelings that we never got around to telling each other what was really on our minds. Whatever it is that we are in the middle of, it's your move. I wish I had done a better job of showing you how important you are to me. If I knew and still truly believed you were always eventually coming home to me like you promised three years ago, I would still be there waiting for you. I only wish you still meant what you said to me so many times. I spent three years believing you, and now I just feel used, like a convenience of some sort you kept in your possession just in case I might be useful one day. I'm sure you have a different view, but it doesn't appear we'll ever find that middle ground again. For such a strong soldier, you gave up in this battle without much of a fight. There are no words to express how sad and hurt I feel by all of this, and I hope one day you are able to once again feel genuine emotions. I love the Rachel I married, but I don't even know you.

Evan

When he finished writing the note, he reread it. He knew no words would really work, but he had written at least part of what he felt, and that was the best he could do. He placed the note on the table along with his room key, picked up his suitcase, and walked out the door. He had to wonder if he was walking away from everything that had been good in his life, and he wanted to cry again but refrained. Between his door and his car, there was a newlywed couple laughing and hugging, and he did not want to ruin their morning.

The two-and-a-half hour drive from Fort Myers to St. Petersburg was an eternity and a blur at the same time. Evan knew he had passed some beautiful sights, but he could not remember any. He arrived at the airport three hours before his flight left for home, so he had more than enough time to return his car and think about how everything in his world had just changed. He bought a newspaper and a paperback and pretended to read them both at various times. His mind raced to a thousand places, but he was unable to focus on any of the thoughts he had. Rachel had surely read his note by now and was undoubtedly working on her reply. For some naïve reason, Evan kept checking his cell phone as if he thought he might have missed a call or a message from her. He had not.

As he sat alone in the terminal, he still searched for answers. How had everything gotten to where it was? Was he completely an impediment and an obstruction that she now thought would prevent her from reaching her new goals, whatever they were? What came next? The answers he had gotten in Fort Myers had only led him to more questions.

Several flights landed while Evan sat and waited for his flight to board, and numerous soldiers had proudly walked through the concourse, each one in uniform, smiling and eager to begin to enjoy some R & R. Under normal circumstances, Evan would have gone out of his way to shake their hands and thank them for their service but not on this day. On this day, he despised the military and all the powers it had to destroy. Its destructive abilities reached far greater distances than the fallout from any bomb it could drop from the sky, and he had now fully felt its effects. He could find nothing inside himself that got him excited about having experienced that.

Finally his flight was called, and he couldn't have been more ready to board the plane. As he took his seat and got settled in, he wondered if anyone could ever start his life over in the same place. Could there really be a "do over" for him? He knew it could not be done without making some major changes, but he believed he could make them. He thought it might be easier to really begin again in a totally different place though, so he started thinking about that and where he could possibly go. Many of the changes he faced had been brought about by others, but the rest of the changes he would have to make on his own. He decided to use his flight time to begin thinking of an acceptable new path for his life.

He would have been willing to fight with all his effort to save his marriage if he had seen even the smallest glimpse that there was a chance it could succeed. The past five months and, in particular, the last day and a half had shown him how fruitless any attempt to do that might be. Rachel had simply turned off the switch and had emotionally left the building. It still stunned him that she could do that with such apparent ease and calm, but that was the military way. Consider your options, weigh all the possible outcomes, and make a decision. Simple.

The world looked so different to Evan from thirty thousand feet above the ground. He could see no tension or conflict or battles. All that lay below him was a beautiful and endless canvass of land and trees and lakes, and it all appeared so tranquil from the viewpoint of his plane seat. He knew his current peaceful view would disappear once his plane landed and he was in his car driving home. When he thought of home, he wondered if it would be better for him to sell the house and truly start over in another town. Most of Rachel's things were already packed and boxed, so separating what belonged to each of them would not be an impossible task. He shook his head and again wondered how it had come to that, and he was amazed at the speed with which it had gotten there.

Evan shivered when he stepped outside the airport, and he knew in an instant he was not in South Florida anymore. He found his car, let it warm up, and then drove home. He knew there would be days ahead that would challenge his emotions, but he felt more mentally prepared than he had before. The questions that had plagued him for so long had, for the most part, been answered, and now he could begin to deal with things instead of always wondering about them. A divorce was never a fun thing for anyone, but he now saw that as an inevitable thing that could not be avoided. When Rachel could not find a reason for him to stay in Florida besides "it's paid for already," he finally felt like he knew where he stood with her. He was done being weak, and once he made that decision, he immediately felt a renewed energy that had been absent inside him for far too long. As he drove along, he wondered if

Jordan would be able to notice his energy as easily as he had noticed his depression. He hoped so.

His house was like a welcome friend even though he had only been gone for two short nights. He unpacked his things and didn't even worry about how the other suitcase would get back home. He figured that either Rachel would mail it to him or her mom would bring it whenever she returned. He really didn't care. He understood that if he was going to make a new start, he needed to begin right away, so he spent the next three hours searching the house for things that belonged to Rachel, and he put everything of hers in an empty bedroom so it would all be together when she wanted to take it all to wherever her army life led her next.

The following day, he put his house up for sale and began searching for a new job with an enthusiasm he had not shown before. He knew he would find something this time, and he knew he would land on his feet. He also knew he had to accept that he might not ever learn all the real reasons why Rachel had chosen the path she had taken or learn what things about him had changed her from a loving wife and teacher to a cold, blunt, dismissive soldier. He understood immediately that not knowing those things would perhaps be the hardest thing for him to deal with in the future.

He could not live as a convenience for anyone, and he would never do that again. His last three years had been miserable, and he had absolutely nothing to show for them. Now it was time to come out of his hibernation and rejoin the world. He could already see a road opening up before him, and though he had no idea where it would take him, he was certainly ready to begin the journey.

Two weeks after he returned from the condo in Florida, Christmas arrived, and it was yet another holiday he spent alone. Toward evening, he checked his e-mail, and to his surprise, there was one from Rachel. He knew she was still in Florida and had not left to return to Iraq yet, so he hesitated briefly and then clicked on it to see what she had written. When he read her message, all he could do was laugh.

She was definitely a soldier. The message showed no emotion, no remorse, no kindness or sadness, and was straight to the point in just a few words.

I'm done. I've decided that I really like being alone.
I'd appreciate it if you'd get all my stuff separated out, and
we can take care of everything when I get back at the end
of my tour.

Me

He was done too, but at least he had tried to explain to her some of what he felt, but she would not do that for him. So be it. Evan looked at the computer screen and renewed his dislike for war. Battles fought in the field could easily be seen, and there could be a winner. The quiet battles at home and in a person's mind that stemmed from the larger war were not as easy to fight or see, and Evan now knew that those battles rarely had winners. There were no heroes here or medals to be presented, just casualties. Nearly everyone involved lost somehow, and he was sorry more people did not understand or realize that. He and Rachel had both lost, for a thousand reasons, and he knew that bell could never be unrung. He knew that while all this was happening to him in the present, it was already time to put the past away and look forward. He closed his e-mail and walked into the kitchen to begin cooking his Christmas dinner, a hamburger that he would eat in front of the television while he sat alone and watched *It's a Wonderful Life.*

CHAPTER 30

Erin listened attentively as Evan tried his best to explain everything he wasn't sure he would be able to tell her. He smiled at her and mischievously commented," I'm impressed you didn't run for the hills in the middle of hearing all that."

She squeezed his hand. "No running away here, and I really do understand most of the reasons behind what you told me. I'm not in a huge hurry to put my heart at risk like that either. However, if you stop taking any risks, you'll spend the rest of your life living in the past, and to me that's the same as not living at all, perhaps even worse."

Evan nodded in agreement. "Wow, you're not only pretty but you're wise too! That's why I'm here, Erin. It's time to start doing more than just breathing. I'm trying my best to try and make a clean break from the life I've been pretending to live and try to get back into the starting blocks and begin a brand new race."

"Sounds like a coach talking there," she grinned.

Evan's problem was not with Erin. He thought she was wonderful. His problem was with himself, and he knew it. The geography between here and home was also a huge hurdle for him. He had made a pact with himself that he would never again be involved in a long-distance relationship because, in his view, it was a recipe for inevitable disappointment. He didn't know if he could ever convince himself to break that rule or not, but he was certain that it would not happen this soon in his new beginning. He did not want to mislead Erin in any way, so he made extra sure she understood how major that was for him. She understood.

The earliest hints of sunrise appeared in the sky, and they realized, to their amazement, that they had spent the entire night on the beach, walking and talking. "Look at that," stated Evan, pointing to the brightening skyline. "You kept me out all night." Neither had worried about time or had even thought about it, but now they were forced to think about the clock as a few joggers began to appear and they no longer had the beach to themselves. They knew others would find their way to the beach soon, and another sunny winter day in Fort Myers would get underway.

Erin and Evan continued walking and slowly made their way back to the Sand Crabbe, the place where their night together had begun many hours earlier, and they both chuckled at the nearly deserted parking lot and the silence that hung over the entire place. "Where did everybody go?" asked Evan without really needing an answer. When they had left, the parking lot was packed, and the club was loud and rowdy, but just before dawn it appeared much more calm and serene.

"Who knows?" replied Erin. "I thought this was a party town. Hard to believe they all went home before sunrise." They both laughed at her statement, but it was also a reminder that the sun was indeed rising, and their time together was growing shorter quickly.

There were only two cars in the parking lot, one with Florida plates and the other a rental, and as they neared the cars, Evan tried to come up with a clever idea for what to do next. Staying up all night had made him hungry, and he took his cue from his stomach. "Are you up for some food? I'm really hungry."

"Sure," she answered. "Food sounds really good. How about the Waffle House? It's right there across the street."

"Sounds perfect," exclaimed Evan.

With renewed energy, Erin took Evan's hand, and they walked across the street. Their cars would be fine where they were a little while longer.

There were a few other customers in the Waffle House, but they were able to find a booth away from the others. The waitress wore a pleasant smile as she greeted Erin and Evan and brought them their menus and their first cups of coffee. It only took a few minutes to decide what they wanted to eat, and after they ordered, they sat looking at each other, smiling through their sleepiness. It was getting lighter by the minute outside, and Evan knew their night together was quickly coming to an end. If he could have pushed back the morning sun, he would have, but he knew better. Time waited for no one, and the best they could do was enjoy the short amount of time they had left together that morning and then see what time and fate had in store for their futures.

Evan and Erin both fought back several yawns while waiting for their breakfast to arrive. Knowing that they were about to lose their battle with time, they didn't waste any of the minutes they had left. Erin sipped her coffee and spoke first. "I really do understand most of what you told me, and I feel basically the same way you do. It wasn't that long ago that I was burned in a relationship, and I'm not in any big hurry to completely put my heart at risk either. When I next give my heart to someone, I want him to be right here near me and not an airport and a jet flight away from me."

Evan smiled as she talked, knowing they were on the same page. He knew he had made a new and special friend, but in a few hours, each of them would return to their own individual reality, and the other would not be a part of that. That knowledge did not reduce the importance of their night together on the beach. It had shown them both that it was all right to once again let down their emotional guard, and they learned once more that life is to be lived and shared and enjoyed, a lesson they had both previously forgotten.

Erin continued, "I want to thank you for last night. It was wonderful and romantic and I needed a night like that."

He grinned at her. "I don't deserve any thanks. I'm the outsider, remember? Your group asked me to join you, and trust me, I'm hugely grateful for all the kindness and patience you showed me. But now I have to go home." Though their parting from each other was imminent, there was no sadness in their breakfast booth. It was all smiles.

Erin and Evan finished their breakfasts, and Evan looked at his watch. "I hate to but I really need to get going or I'll miss my flight." He was as comfortable with her as he had been with Rachel in the beginning of their relationship, and that realization made him squirm just a little in his seat. He was not ready for another relationship yet, but he was closer than he had been at the start of the weekend, and he knew he would get there sooner rather than later.

"I know," she replied softly. "You have to go."

They walked across the street to their cars, and they stood together, leaning on Erin's car. He put his arm around her, and she leaned against him, sharing what they knew was probably a final hug. Evan smiled broadly. "I just want to tell you again how glad I am to have found you and how important last night was to me."

Rachel smiled back at him. "I'm glad too, and last night was just as important to me."

"I don't have a crystal ball," continued Evan. "There might come a day when this can all work out, and I'm sure it could be amazing, but today is not that day."

"Have a great flight," she beamed, "and keep smiling."

"Keep smiling," he replied. "I like that. Now that I've found my smile again, I'm going to be using it a lot."

They embraced tightly, just as Evan and Rachel had done before she boarded her plane to deploy, and then they said good-bye. He got into his car and drove away from a woman who, in less than twenty-four hours, had become a very important part of his life. His weekend of clearing his head had come to an end, and he realized that his goal had been reached. For the first time in a very long time, he really felt like he could leave a lot of his baggage behind and move on. He knew it was time to do that, and at last, he felt like he could.